A RECIPE FOR DEATH

A Down South Café Mystery

Gayle Leeson

Grace Abraham Publishing
Bristol, Virginia

Dedicated to Tim, Lianna, and Nicholas

Chapter One

It was immediately apparent that Walter and Dilly weren't their normal, chipper selves. They were whispering to each other as they came through the door and continued to do so as they sat at their favorite table. Usually our first customers of the day, the lively duet typically already knew what they wanted for breakfast and were eager to chat with us as we prepared their meals.

"Is everything all right?" I asked.

Nudging Walter, Dilly said, "Tell them."

"Why do I have to tell them?" Walter looked more like a petulant child than a man in his eighties. "You tell them. Besides, it looked as if we were interrupting a serious conversation among the kids when we walked in."

The "kids" were Jackie, Scott, and me. I'd recently made Jackie and Scott my partners in the café.

"We weren't having that serious of a discussion," I said. "We were simply speculating about the recent decline in business. Do you think customers might be getting bored with our recipes?"

"Not at all!" Dilly gave her husband another nudge. "Tell them."

He took a deep breath. "I saw a food truck parked near Poston's bookstore yesterday."

"He said it was called Better'n Yer Mama's," Dilly said.

"Who's operating this food truck?" Jackie asked. "And why would our patrons betray us to go running to them?"

"What are they serving?" Scott asked.

"Apparently, they serve something different every day," Walter said.

Speaking loudly enough to be heard over Jackie's sputtering, I said, "So, there's a food truck in town. That's good. Maybe we needed a little healthy competition to get us back on our toes."

"That's the spirit." Scott grinned. "We won't let them get us down. Maybe we should do a little more promotion...offer a special deal every Friday on social media or something."

"That's a good idea," Dilly said. "Walter and I will do some recon at lunchtime and see what they're serving today."

"If the truck is still around after the café closes, I might go by there and say hello," I said. "I'm really curious about it."

"I'm more than curious." Jackie was fuming. "I want to see their business license, their health permit, their food handler certification, and their zoning approval. This truck might not even be legal." She turned to me. "You need to get your fiancé on this pronto."

My fiancé, Ryan, was a deputy.

"No, I need to get back to work and make breakfast for our two best customers." I smiled at Dilly and Walter. "What'll it be today?"

After volleying their options back and forth for a moment, they both chose eggs, bacon, biscuits, and pancakes.

"We have some freshly made strawberry preserves," I said. "Would Buddy like some on his biscuit today?"

Buddy was a raccoon who came down out of the woods behind their house to get a biscuit every evening. We were all guilty of spoiling the little critter.

"We'd better stick with peanut butter." Dilly shook her head. "The last time we tried something different, he acted plumb mad."

"He still ate it, but, boy, did he chitter and chatter about it." Walter chuckled. "I'd sure like some of those strawberry preserves, though."

"Me too," Dilly said. "And a jar to go if you can spare it."

"Always." I gave her a smile as I went into the kitchen and got to work.

Scott followed me and began mixing up pancake batter. "You all right, Amy-girl?"

"I'm fine." I slid a pan of biscuits into the oven and put the bacon and eggs onto the griddle. "The food truck threw me, that's all. I don't know why. They're really popular. Why *shouldn't* there be a food truck in Winter Garden?"

"True, but we were all so used to the café and the pizza parlor being the only two restaurants in Winter Garden," he said. "And everybody in town was used to that too."

"Yeah." I sighed. "Maybe it's only a spring and summer thing, and they'll move on when it starts getting cooler. I mean, it's April, and there's still a nip in the air. Who'd want to eat outside in the cold?"

"I imagine most people get their food to go. Either way, we're going to be fine."

As we continued preparing Walter and Dilly's orders, I prayed Scott was right. Had I bitten off more than I could chew at one time? I'd invited Scott and Jackie to become partners in the business, plus Ryan and I were planning on getting married when the lease on his apartment was up this fall. It gave us plenty of time to work out all the arrangements, but it was a huge step. Everything was changing so quickly. And now there was a food truck hanging around. I was afraid that if it became too popular, the Down South Café might not survive.

I'd worked hard to build up the café's reputation and clientele since I'd bought and renovated the place. The once ugly linoleum had been replaced with beautiful bamboo flooring, and the dingy brown and orange décor were now cheery yellow and blue. The cumbersome booths had made way for bistro tables and wrought-iron chairs.

I loved this place. The only reason I'd brought Scott and Jackie on as partners was because Ryan had asked me to marry him a few months earlier, and

I'd realized I'd need to pull back on my workload a little when we decided to start a family. Plus, Scott and Jackie were dedicated to the café, and they deserved the opportunity to be a bigger part of it.

Homer Pickens came in at ten-thirty a.m. for his sausage biscuit. You could have set your watch by Homer. If he'd ever missed his standing breakfast appointment by more than ten minutes either way, I'd have sent out a search party. Immediately. And if he ever ordered anything other than a sausage biscuit, I'd call for an ambulance.

"Good morning, Homer." I poured him a cup of coffee. "Who's your hero today?"

Homer chose a different hero each day. As a man in his mid- to late-sixties, he was bound to be running out of heroes. But he showed no sign of slowing down.

"Walter Elias Disney, who—contrary to persistent rumors—was not cryogenically frozen but who does hold the record for the most Oscar wins—22–and nominations—59."

"How very impressive," I said.

"Yes, and I admire the fact that he overcame many obstacles and setbacks," Homer said. "Mr. Disney is quoted as saying, 'I decided to see every problem as an opportunity to find a solution.'"

"Good advice and timely as well." I told him that we'd learned this morning that a food truck was in town.

"They're poaching our customers," Jackie said.

"They aren't getting my business." Homer raised his coffee cup to his lips. "I'd never go anywhere else. This food truck thing is a passing fancy." He took a sip before returning the cup to its saucer. "People will get tired of it and return to the café."

"Thank you for your insights and your loyalty, Homer." I smiled. "I don't wish the food truck any ill will, though. I feel like there's room for everyone, especially here in Winter Garden where there are so few dining options."

"Mr. Disney would be proud of you." Homer lifted his cup in a salute. "He once said, 'I have been up against tough competition all my life. I wouldn't know how to get along without it.' And, as you know, he turned out all right."

"He sure did. As did you." I jerked my head toward the kitchen. "I'd better get your sausage biscuit ready."

I didn't look in Jackie's direction as I went into the kitchen, but I could feel the heat of her glare. While I understood that she was invested in the café's success like never before since becoming a partner, so were Scott and I. And we would work together to make it prosper.

But the key phrase was *work together.*

Dilly and Walter came back after the lunch rush, which was admittedly less rushed than usual.

"We went to the food truck," Dilly said.

"The one called Better'n Yer Mama's." Walter provided that unnecessary detail as if Winter Garden had enjoyed a sudden influx of food trucks. "The food was good. It didn't compare to your food, Amy, but it wasn't bad."

"Today was specialty taco day." Dilly took a seat at the counter. "I had a fish taco, which is something I'd never had before."

Walter remained standing and lightly placed his hands on Dilly's shoulders. "I had a steak taco with onions, cheese, lettuce, tomato, and sour cream."

"Sounds good," Scott said.

"Oh, it was."

Dilly turned to frown up at him.

"Um, but it wasn't as good as tacos we'd get here, I'm sure," Walter added.

"Tomorrow, we should make tacos our special of the day," Jackie said.

"No, we've already bought all the ingredients for tomorrow's special—chicken pot pie—so that's what we'll be having," I said.

"Chicken pot pie sounds good," Dilly said. "Better than the chicken and waffles the food truck will be serving."

Walter's expression said that was debatable, but he wisely refrained from commenting.

"I'd like to go ahead and put in a request for tomorrow," Dilly said. "Not chicken pot pie, though. We're heading to Biltmore for the day, and I'd like you to pack up Walter and me some ham biscuits and pastries for the road."

"We'll do that," I said.

"If you'll give me your pastry preferences, I'll make sure you have what you'd like," Scott said.

"I would adore a cheese Danish," Walter said.

"You've got it, my man."

"And I'll make sure there's a plain biscuit wrapped separately for Buddy," I said.

"You're too good to us." Dilly stood. "No food truck will ever take your place."

"As I told Homer Pickens earlier today, there's room for some healthy competition." I grinned. "We can handle it."

Walter and Dilly left, and our lone customer finished his meal, paid, and left as well.

With the café empty, Jackie turned on me. "Am I a true partner in this business or not?"

"Of course, you are. So is Scott."

"Then why don't we get a say in what goes on around here?" Jackie asked.

"You do get a say. The three of us sat down and worked out this week's menu specials after the café closed on Saturday," I said. "We can't throw our plans out the window on a Wednesday simply because a food truck has moved into Winter Garden."

"Amy's right," Scott said. "Letting the food we bought for the week go to waste would hurt our bottom line a lot more than losing a few customers."

"Chicken pot pie can't compete with chicken and waffles." Jackie flounced into the kitchen.

I looked at Scott, and he merely shrugged.

"It'll be all right," he said softly. "She just needs to simmer down."

I wasn't so sure it would be all right. In fact, I hoped that making my cousin a partner in the Down South Café wouldn't turn out to have been an enormous mistake.

Chapter Two

As soon as the café closed and the clean up was finished, I went to check out the Better'n Yer Mama's food truck for myself. That afternoon, it was parked in the square outside the municipal building that housed the sheriff's office, the post office, and the mayor's office.

I parked, got out of my yellow VW "bug," and approached the truck.

"Hello, young lady! Are you lookin' for the best taco you've ever put in your mouth?"

Smiling at the bear of a man standing at the counter, I said, "Not at the moment. I just wanted to come by and say hello."

"I'm glad you did." He gave me a wide grin and shoved his rolled-up flannel shirt sleeves farther up his muscled forearms. "But I bet I can change your mind. Come here and taste this steak."

"You make a tempting offer, Mr.—"

"Wood Bradford. And you are?"

"Amy Flowers. I run the Down South Café." I held out my hand for him to shake. "Welcome to Winter Garden. I'm hearing rave reviews about your food truck."

"Glad to hear it. Hope I'm not putting too much of a dent in your bottom line."

"Of course, you aren't."

He looked a little crestfallen to hear that, but he recovered quickly. "Well, that's good. I was afraid you might be coming to ask me to park my truck in another town."

"Absolutely not, Mr. Bradford. I think it's great that Winter Garden residents now have three dining options rather than two." I laughed. "It's been us and the pizza parlor for ages. It's nice to have you here."

"I appreciate that, Amy, and please call me Wood—short for Woodrow, named after my daddy's daddy. I'm relieved we're not going to be enemies. I might even stop by the café sometime."

"Please do. If I didn't already have plans for dinner, I'd certainly take you up on that offer of a taco. I've heard they're delicious." I jerked my head in the direction of the police station. "I'd better get going. I hope to see you again."

"Likewise. Have a good evenin'."

I walked into the police station, and several officers guiltily tried to hide their taco wrappers. I wanted to tell them it was no big deal, but I was afraid it would only make matters worse. Ryan wasn't at his desk, so I sat on the chair in front of it to wait for him.

Sheriff Billings poked his head out of his office and asked me to come talk with him. When I got inside and took a seat, he closed the door.

"You look concerned," he said, sitting back down at his desk. "Are you worried about this food truck? I've already checked, and he has all the proper permits."

"Aw, I'm not upset about the food truck. If the Down South Café can't handle a little healthy competition, then we must not have much of a business. I'd hate to think diners frequented the café just because they don't have anywhere else to go."

"I can assure you that people visit your café because the food is delicious."

"Thanks, Sheriff." I took a deep breath. "What I'm concerned about is Jackie. I don't know whether or not you're aware of it, but I offered Jackie and Scott partnerships in the café because they work hard, I wanted them to understand how valuable they are to me, and I wanted them to have a vested interest in the café—to help build something we can all be proud of."

"And now you're regretting going into business with a family member?"

"I wasn't. Until today." I told him about the argument Jackie and I had earlier. "Scott took my side because—well, because I was right. We can't change horses in the middle of the stream simply because there's a food truck in town. She's making a bigger deal out of it than it needs to be."

"Naturally, she doesn't see it that way."

"No. Furthermore, she got upset and accused me of still running the business even though she and Scott are my partners now."

He leaned back in his chair. "It's awfully hard to let go of the reins of something you've put so much of yourself into."

"I know."

"Is it possible you moved into the partnership too quickly?"

"I didn't think so. I considered it carefully before I made them the offer," I said.

"But the new partnership and the engagement...that's a lot of pressure to take on all at once. Even good pressure is pressure, kiddo."

"I know. But what's done is done. Between you and me, I might've been better off partnering only with Scott. For all his laid-back ways, he has a real head for business, and he has grown the bakery considerably."

"Do you think you could buy back Jackie's share of the business?"

"No!" My eyes widened. "I mean, she's my cousin and my best friend. Trying to buy back her share would cause an irreparable rift. Plus, can you imagine how ticked Aunt Bess would be?"

Aunt Bess was my great-aunt, but she was Jackie's grandmother. Granddaughter trumps niece every time.

"Can you reason with her?" Sheriff Billings asked. "Jackie, I mean. I know there's no reasoning with Bess."

"I'll try. But not until tomorrow. Maybe she'll sleep on it and come back in the morning with a clearer head." I wasn't going to hold my breath, but I could hope. I stood. "Thanks for listening."

"Anytime."

I left the sheriff's office and was glad to see that Ryan was at his desk. Joining him, I said, "Hi, there."

"Hi, yourself. Everything okay?" He glanced toward the sheriff's office.

"Yeah. Your boss was giving me a pep talk. He thought I might be concerned about the food truck, but I met Mr. Bradford and welcomed him to the neighborhood."

Ryan laughed. "Of course, you did. Was he nice to you?"

"He was. Although I do think that at first he was a little hurt that I wasn't there to tell him 'this town ain't big enough for the both of us.' He even said he might come by the café sometime."

"Good for him. And especially good for you for making the first move and welcoming him to town." He gazed at me for a moment. "You've got something on your mind, though. What is it?"

"It's nothing—a little spat with Jackie is all. It'll work itself out. I came by to invite you to dinner."

"I'll be there."

Not wanting to interfere with his job, I kept my visit brief.

As I pulled out of my parking spot, I used the hands-free function in my car to call Roger. Roger was not only a childhood friend and Jackie's boy-friend, but he was also a skilled carpenter who owned his own construction company.

"What's up, Flowerpot?"

He was the only person to have ever gotten away with calling me by that nickname. "What're you going to call me when my last name isn't Flowers anymore?"

"I don't care what your name is," he answered. "You'll always be Flowerpot to me."

"Could you come by the house sometime soon? Sometime when Ryan won't be there?"

"Oooh, that's how rumors get started." He chuckled. "I can swing by there in a few minutes if that works for you. I'm on a supply run. We'll have to make it quick though."

"That works great. Thanks, Roger."

I arrived home and greeted Rory, my little brown terrier, who got an instant case of the zoomies and began running all over the house. Princess Eloise, the white Persian that I'd inherited when my mom had gone to live with Aunt Bess, flicked her tail dispassionately.

"Hello, Princess Eloise."

More tail flicking.

Roger arrived and tapped on the door.

"Come on in," I called.

"What's going on?" he asked.

Giving a little sigh, I said, "Follow me."

"That sounds foreboding."

He followed me into the room that had once been my mom's bedroom. After she'd moved into the big house—which was on the hill above my house—with Aunt Bess, I had Roger convert the bedroom into my "fancy room." He'd added floor-to-ceiling book-shelves, and he'd helped me find a reasonably priced roll-top desk. I'd added a white chaise, a peacock blue chair with a matching ottoman, and a reading lamp. It was perfect.

"When Ryan and I get married, he'll be moving in with me and will need a space of his own," I said.

His jaw dropped. "You're giving up your fancy room?"

"I don't want to give it up entirely, but I'd like to divide the room into his and her offices—maybe with some sort of divider between them."

"Wouldn't it be easier to simply build onto the house? We could do it up right all at once," he said. "An office for Ryan, a formal dining room, a nursery, an extra bedroom."

"Um, you're getting a little ahead of yourself." I gave a soft laugh. "I mean, yeah, those things would be great, but no, it wouldn't be simpler to do all that."

Grinning, he said, "Fair point." He took a notebook and pencil from his pocket and removed the tape measure he had clipped to his belt and began measuring and taking notes.

"I want the renovation to be a surprise for Ryan, so when you have your ideas and your estimate, will you share them with me privately?"

"Of course." He returned the notebook to his pocket. "What's up with this food truck?"

Sighing, I said, "I don't know why Jackie is so up in the air about it. She went a little crazy when Dilly and Walter mentioned it today. I tried to tell her it's not a big deal, but that only made matters worse."

"She's probably scared. She's awfully protective of the café."

"Do you think she's having second thoughts about the partnership?" I asked.

"I don't believe so, but I know it was a big step for her. And you know as well as I do that Jackie tends to overthink everything."

"Don't I know it? Maybe you can talk to her about the food truck and convince her that a little competition isn't the end of the world?"

He shook his head. "No thanks, Flowerpot. I don't want her mad at me too."

After he left, I sank onto the chaise to relax for a few minutes. I hadn't meant to doze off and didn't realize I had until I was awakened by my phone ringing.

Looking at the screen, I saw it was Aunt Bess. "Aunt Bess, is everything okay?"

"No," she said. "But don't you give that food truck another thought. I'm going undercover."

Chapter Three

Over a dinner of spaghetti and meatballs, I told Ryan about the phone call from Aunt Bess. "She said she was going undercover!"

He thought it was funny. I did not.

"I told her not to do anything rash. And she said, 'Ooh, a rash. That's good, Amy. I'll pretend I got a rash from his food.' There was no talking her out of whatever it is she plans to do."

"Would you like for me to try to persuade Aunt Bess that the Sheriff's Department has the situation under control?" Ryan asked.

"I doubt it would do any good." I used my fork to twirl my spaghetti into the bowl of my spoon. "Sheriff Billings has already checked and said that the food truck's permits are all in order."

"Does Aunt Bess know that?"

Meeting his eyes, I said, "No. At least, she didn't hear it from me."

"Then letting her think we're on the case might buy some time for her—and maybe even Jackie—to get over the mad spell."

After dinner, we tidied the kitchen and walked up the hill to the big house. Even though I'd worn a jacket, I shivered in the cold night air, and Ryan put his arm around me. We entered the house through the back door, which led to Mom's kitchen.

Mom was sitting at the kitchen table doing a crossword puzzle. "This is a nice surprise."

"From the call I got earlier from Aunt Bess, I'm guessing Jackie stopped by," I said.

"Yep. Stayed long enough to work Aunt Bess up into a tizzy over this food truck business, and then she left."

"I don't know why Jackie is making such a big deal about the food truck." I rubbed my forehead.

"Me either, but she's really lit a fire under Aunt Bess," Mom said.

Entering the kitchen in time to hear the word fire, Aunt Bess said, "That's another thing! The firefighters ate from that godawful food truck today. As good as I've been to them, and they turn their backs on my granddaughter and my niece." She nodded at Ryan and me. "Hi, kids."

"Hello, Aunt Bess," Ryan said.

"Hi," I said. "You know, the firefighters aren't turning their backs on—"

Aunt Bess continued as if I'd never spoken. "And the name—Better'n Yer Mama's!" She harrumphed. "It might be better than your mama's—no offense, Jenna—but I highly doubt it would even come close to my mama's cooking. I'll be telling them that tomorrow."

"Now, Aunt Bess, I don't want you to worry your pretty little head about this food truck."

I thought it was brilliant of Ryan to appeal to Aunt Bess's vanity.

"Let the Sheriff's Department handle the situation for now," he continued.

"Oh, honey, they're handling the situation all right," Aunt Bess said. "They got food from that truck today too—posted about it on social media like it was some kind of big deal."

"I met the proprietor today," I told her. "He seemed nice. I even invited him to come to the Down South Café sometime."

She nodded hard enough to set her tight white curls to bouncing. "Atta girl. Show him you're not a bit afraid of him."

"Exactly." Maybe she was about to see the light. "I'm not afraid of him or intimidated by his business. After all, we go to the pizza parlor sometimes."

Flicking her hand as if she were shooing away a fly, Aunt Bess said, "That's different."

"How is it different?" Mom asked.

"I don't know, but it just is." Aunt Bess pressed her lips together as if there was nothing more to say on the matter.

As far as I was concerned, there wasn't anything more to say.

And then Mom's boyfriend, Clark, arrived. Clark was the only doctor in Winter Garden, and he was often busy until late in the evening.

Mom got up and hugged him hello. "We have left-overs from dinner. I'll be happy to warm them up for you."

"I appreciate that, darling, but I'm still full from lunch. I had the best tacos—"

"Good seeing you, Clark," I interrupted.

"Yeah, man, see you soon." Ryan took my hand and propelled me toward the door.

Once we were safely out of earshot of the house, or more particularly, Aunt Bess, we burst into laughter. We were still laughing when we got back down the long driveway to my place.

Rory raced through the doggie door to greet us from the fenced backyard. His barking made it sound as if he were laughing along with us, which made us laugh harder.

"Clark has no idea about the hornets' nest he poked," Ryan said.

"I'm sure he does by now." I opened the gate, and we went in through the back door.

Rory went back inside with us and retrieved a ball for Ryan to throw for him. Not to be outdone, Princess Eloise wound around Ryan's feet and gazed up at him adoringly. Besides Mom, Ryan was her favorite person. Never mind that I fed her, cuddled her, and gave her treats. Fickle feline.

"Want something to drink?" I asked, taking a bottle of water from the refrigerator.

"I'll take one of those." He tossed the ball for Rory and then scooped Princess Eloise up into his arms.

I could hear her purring from across the room. As I crossed the room with the bottles of water, Rory ran back to drop the sopping wet ball at Ryan's feet. Ryan pulled out a chair and sat down so he could keep Princess Eloise on his lap while still playing with Rory. Kinda feeling like one of Cinderella's ugly stepsisters, I sat down at the other end of the table.

"Are you going to be happy living so close to Mom and Aunt Bess?" I asked. "We could always rent out this house and move."

"Moving to a larger place might be worth considering in the future, but right now I'll be perfectly happy to live here. Will you?"

"Well, yeah, but I've lived here all my life."

He threw the ball again, wiped his hand on the side of his jeans, and looked at me. "Do you feel it's time for a change?"

"No. This little house has everything I need. Or it will when you move in."

Smiling, he said, "That's all I need to know."

"Are you going to miss your apartment?" I asked.

"No." He rubbed Princess Eloise's chin.

"We could always ask Roger to build an addition onto the house if you need more space."

Ryan placed Princess Eloise onto the floor and ignored Rory's latest silent plea for attention. He came over, took me by the shoulders, and said, "Please stop worrying. I'd hate to think Aunt Bess would try to go undercover and spy on us because she's afraid you're dissatisfied."

I stood, took his hand, and led him into the living room where I sank onto the sofa. "Do you think it's the food truck that's upsetting Jackie, or is it the fact that Scott and I didn't go along with her suggestion that we change up our specials?"

"Maybe she had something else on her mind altogether—like a spat with Roger."

Shaking my head, I said, "I don't think so. He didn't mention anything about a spat." I realized Ryan didn't know Roger had been here today. "I spoke with him about Jackie's outburst. He told me she wants to help the café succeed now more than ever. I get that, but the three of us have to work as a team."

"That can be hard to do sometimes."

"I know, especially for Jackie."

He laughed softly. "Not just Jackie."

"What? I can be a team player. I can! Scott and I understand each other well."

"Do you? Or does Scott defer to you because he still considers you his boss?"

"Of course, he doesn't," I said. "He understands that when you make a plan, you stick to it. Next week, we'll make a new plan, but the one in place this week can't be altered simply because a food truck has rolled into town. Right? I mean, that's Business 101, isn't it?"

"It is." He spread his hands. "All I'm saying is that the three of you have to come to grips with your new roles at the café, and there are going to be learning curves and growing pains."

"I know." I snuggled close to him. "Let's watch some silly sitcom. I don't want to think about work anymore until tomorrow morning. And I definitely don't want to contemplate what Aunt Bess might get up to."

Chapter Four

While I knew better than to hope my eyes were deceiving me, I turned to Scott and quietly asked, "That is Aunt Bess coming in here wearing that baseball cap and sunglasses, isn't it?"

"Absolutely, Amy-girl." He laughed. "And your mom looks as happy about the situation as you do."

Mom was trudging along behind Aunt Bess as if she'd rather be anywhere else.

Hurrying to open the door for them, Scott said, "Aunt Bess, you're looking pretty as a picture. You aren't scheduled to throw out the first pitch of the game somewhere, are you?"

"Thank you, darlin'. I'm not supposed to throw out any first pitch, but I could and would if somebody would ask me." She patted his face gently. "If you hear of anybody needing a ceremonial first pitch thrown, tell 'em to call me."

"You know I will." He grinned. "So, what's with the cap and glasses?"

"I'm going undercover today." She walked over to the counter and took a seat beside Homer Pickens. "Mornin', Homer."

"Howdy, Miss Bess."

Mom sat at a table as far away from Aunt Bess as she could get. I took her a cup of coffee.

"Can I get you anything else?" I asked.

"A cinnamon roll and a few minutes' peace?"

"I can get you the cinnamon roll." I patted her shoulder. "I'll heat it in the microwave for a few seconds so it'll be extra yummy."

"Thanks."

"Who's your hero today, Homer?" Aunt Bess asked.

"It's Muhammad Ali, the heavyweight boxing champion."

"I could use me some of that Ali muscle and wit today," she said. "I'm looking for that food truck that's been horning in on the café's business."

Jackie set a cup of coffee in front of her grandmother. "Then turn around, Granny. It's in our parking lot."

"What!" Aunt Bess nearly spilled the coffee in her haste to turn around.

For the second time in a matter of minutes, I wished my eyes were deceiving me. But nope. There was the Better'n Yer Mama's food truck sitting at the far end of our parking lot, and Woodrow Bradford was climbing down out of the driver's seat.

"Well, what do you know?" Homer was the first to speak. And it might've been all right had he stopped there; but, of course, he didn't. "He surely doesn't have the audacity to set up right in the parking lot, does he?"

"He'd better not," Jackie said. "If he does, he'll regret it."

"That reminds me of a Muhammad Ali quote," Homer said. "He said, 'If you even dream of beating me, you'd better wake up and apologize.' That's pretty good, huh?"

"Not helping," I mumbled.

I took Mom's warm cinnamon roll to her and walked closer to the door to head off Mr. Bradford's being met by the delegation of grandmother and granddaughter mountain lions.

"Good morning, Mr. Bradford," I said as he walked through the door. "Nice to see you again."

"Hey, there, Amy. I'm taking you up on your offer to stop by. And please call me 'Wood.' I thought we got the formalities out of the way yesterday."

"Of course. What can I get for you, Wood?"

"I've been hearing particularly good things about the café's desserts," he said.

"Well, then, let me introduce you to Scott. He makes the majority of our pastries." I motioned to Scott, and he came over. "Scott, this is Wood Bradford. He said he's heard a lot of good things about our desserts."

Scott shook Mr. Bradford's hand. "Glad to hear it."

"I don't offer desserts from the food truck—I own and operate Better'n Yer Mama's—and I'm beginning to realize that's a shortcoming. May I?" He pointed toward the dessert case.

"Sure." Scott walked Mr. Bradford over to the dessert case.

As Mr. Bradford perused the dessert case, Aunt Bess and Jackie looked from him to each other with undisguised irritation. Homer looked curious. Luis ventured out of the kitchen with apparent concern.

And Mom merely ate her cinnamon roll as if she were in her own, private happy place.

Mr. Bradford ordered a cinnamon roll, a cream-filled cupcake, and a chocolate chunk peanut butter cookie. Scott didn't go into any of the particulars about how the treats were made, as he normally would have with a patron who was gushing over his desserts. Instead, he got the man a cup of coffee.

After taking a bite of each of the confections, Mr. Bradford said, "These are delicious. I'll take a dozen of each."

"What are you up to?" Jackie asked him.

"I'm going to offer them to my customers today." Mr. Bradford smiled at her.

She didn't smile back. "That's what I figured, and I don't appreciate it."

He fished a card from his jacket pocket. It had been ornately printed with, "Desserts Created by the Down South Café."

"Fair enough," Scott said. "It'll be good advertising."

"I agree." Smiling at Mr. Bradford, I said, "Thank you for your business and word of mouth."

"I won't mark 'em up but a teensy bit." He winked. "And I'll let everybody know I tried them all before passing them along." He nodded toward the cupcake and the cinnamon roll. "Could I get you to put those in a box for me please? I'm going to finish the cookie."

I packed the cupcake and cinnamon roll along with napkins and a plastic fork into a box. "I hope you'll enjoy these later."

"You know I will. If this goes as well as I believe it will, I'll see you again in the morning." He took his box, along with the boxes of cupcakes, cinnamon rolls, and cookies that Scott had packed up, and left.

"He's got a lot of nerve," Jackie said. "Waltzing in here as if we're all buddies and buying up the majority of our cookies and cupcakes."

"But it's okay since he's giving the café credit for making the desserts, right?" Luis asked. "It's like we're in two places at once today."

"It's only okay if he does give the café credit," Aunt Bess said. "And I'll see to it that he does." She slid off her stool. "Come on, Jenna. We need to follow that food truck."

"Nope. I'm not spending my day chasing down a food truck," Mom said. "I'm going to Bristol to do some shopping. You're welcome to come with me, or I can drop you back off at home."

Aunt Bess pressed her lips into a thin line. "I'm not going home. I'm going to find that food truck and make sure that Woody person is giving credit where credit is due even if I have to walk."

"I don't mind driving you, Miss Bess," Homer said. "We'll find out where the truck has gone, give him time to set up, and make sure he's doing right by the café. Then I can take you home."

"Well, I am in your debt!" Aunt Bess looked around at the rest of us. "We all are."

Homer paid for his breakfast, and he and Aunt Bess left.

Mom rolled her eyes. "You know how Batman and Robin are called the 'dynamic duo'? Well, there goes the dangerous duo."

"Or, at the very least, the disturbing duo," I said.

Scott shook his head. "The destructive duo."

Mom, Luis, and I agreed. Jackie didn't comment. She simply turned and went into the kitchen.

"Do you need any help replenishing the dessert case before the lunch rush?" Mom asked.

"No, thank you," I said. "We have everything under control. Go and enjoy yourself."

"Yes." Scott patted her shoulder. "Enjoy every second before Aunt Bess calls you to come bail her out of jail."

Ivy, Scott's sister and the region's foremost crime scene technician, came into the café for lunch. We were busy, but not as busy as we usually were in the middle of the week.

Taking a seat at the counter, she blew out a breath. "That big ugly food truck is set up in the municipal parking lot again today, which makes it awfully hard for those of us who actually have to get in and out of the parking lot to do so without hitting anyone."

"If it's causing trouble for people getting in and out of the lot, you'd think the sheriff would ask that it be moved," I said. "Iced tea?"

"Please. Thanks, Amy." She shook her head. "Maybe I'm just irritable today. I suppose some people enjoy having a lunch that's right outside their door where they can simply walk outside, buy food, and take it back to their desks or break rooms. Not me. When I take lunch, I want to get as far away from work as possible."

"I understand that." I poured her tea over a glass of ice and placed it in front of her. "What would you like to eat?"

"Definitely not chicken and waffles." She gave me a wry smile. "How about a chicken Caesar salad?"

"Coming right up." I went into the kitchen to get started on the salad.

Jackie, who'd overheard my conversation with Ivy, glared at me as I walked into the kitchen. She must've heard my telepathic plea of don't start because she didn't say anything.

Scott brought another order to the window. "I asked Ivy if Aunt Bess has been arrested yet. She said no, so that's good news."

"Unless she and Homer have gone on the run." I put grilled chicken in Ivy's salad.

"No way. Homer has to be here on time to get his sausage biscuit in the morning," Scott said, before going back to check on his customers.

"This is all a big joke to you two, isn't it?" Jackie asked, as she flipped burgers on the grill.

"It's not a joke, Jackie, but what are we going to do about it?" I added croutons and dressing before taking the salad out to Ivy.

When I returned to the kitchen, Luis, who was refilling ketchup dispensers, said, "If I heard her correctly, Ivy said the main draw of the food truck is that it's handy. Maybe the Down South Café could start offering delivery? I mean, I don't know, but—"

Scott brought another order to the window in time to hear what Luis said. "Way to think proactively, bro. We'll give it some thought."

I appreciated that Luis had noticed the tension among us and hoped to help alleviate it in some way, but meal delivery wasn't a viable option for us right now. We'd have to hire a delivery person, get extra insurance for that person driving to and from the café to customers' homes or businesses, and I had no idea what other considerations might have to be taken.

Jackie exclaimed, "What?"

Turning to see who she was addressing, I saw that she still had her back to Luis and me. She was apparently talking with someone through her headset.

"On my way." She walked over, handed me her spatula, and took off her apron. "I've got to go. Granny is in trouble."

"What's going on?" I asked.

"I don't know. She just said she's in trouble and needs me to come and get her."

"Where? What about Homer?"

Jackie didn't answer me as she hurried out of the café.

Chapter Five

Luis and I were on pins and needles as we finished out the day, but Scott was his typical easygoing self.

"It's all good," he told us. "Aunt Bess might've gotten herself into a little hot water, but I'm sure it's nothing Jackie can't get her out of."

"But what kind of hot water? And will we be able to get Jackie out of any hot water she gets into?" I cleaned the front door glass. "And why didn't Jackie at least let us know what's going on?"

I was afraid I already knew the answer to that—Jackie was so angry with me that she wouldn't even let me know if Aunt Bess was okay. I hadn't alerted Mom because I knew she'd have let me know if she'd heard anything And I liked to think Mom was enjoying herself while out shopping. She didn't get very many days to enjoy all to herself.

Mom had given up her retail work when she'd moved into the big house to care for Aunt Bess after Nana's death. Not that Aunt Bess needed full-time care by any stretch of the imagination, but she certainly couldn't live on her own. I shuddered to think of what my great-aunt would get into if left to her own devices.

Aunt Bess was known for her Pinterest boards: Lord, Have Mercy; Things I'd Like to Eat but Won't Make; People I've Outlived; Crime Scenes; and Things That'll Probably Kill Me. If she lived alone, she could probably add: Things I Set on Fire so the Firefighters Would Come; Buttons I Probably Shouldn't Have Pushed; and People I've Catfished.

She might already have enough pins to get a good start on that Catfished board, although as far as I knew, she'd only used my mom's information and profile picture to set up that one date. Mom had not been amused. Neither had the man who'd thought he had a date to a dance with Mom rather than Aunt Bess.

I'd finished cleaning the door and windows and was looking around to see what else needed to be done when I saw Ryan pulling into the parking lot in his police cruiser. My heart plummeted. He was still on duty. Was this visit official?

Scott and Luis obviously shared my fear that something bad had happened. Before Ryan even got out of the car, the two of them were standing on either side of me. Did they expect me to faint? I wasn't typically a fainter. Still, it was nice to have their support.

"Aunt Bess is all right," Ryan said, as he opened the door.

"What happened?" I asked.

He walked to the nearest table, pulled out a chair, and sank onto it. Luis and I joined him at the table. Scott flipped over the "closed" sign, locked the door, and then took a seat.

Taking a deep breath, I said, "Tell us what she did."

"She sneaked into the Better'n Yer Mama's bathroom and hid," Ryan said.

Luis couldn't manage to stifle a chuckle. "Sorry."

"Has she been arrested for trespassing?" I asked.

"No. I'm only guessing she sneaked into the food truck." Ryan ran a hand through his hair. "It's possible Mr. Bradford invited her in."

"Can't you ask Mr. Bradford?" Scott asked quietly.

Ryan shook his head. "He's still unconscious and might not wake up."

My hand flew to my throat. "Please tell me Aunt Bess didn't hit him over the head or something."

"She didn't," he said. "In fact, no one even knew she was in the truck until we had it towed to our impound lot. Then she came staggering out saying the ride made her dizzy, and she called Jackie."

At this, both Luis and Scott burst out laughing. They appeared to have missed the important information about Mr. Bradford being unconscious.

"So what happened to Mr. Bradford, and where is Homer?" I asked.

"Homer and Aunt Bess are at the police station," Ryan said. "Aunt Bess is being questioned. Homer is in the clear. He'd gone into the post office to buy stamps, had struck up a conversation with a Mr. Fremont, who was mailing a package to his daughter, and hadn't been aware of Aunt Bess's disappearance until he heard the commotion around the food truck."

I pinched the bridge of my nose. "I take it the commotion was whatever happened to Mr. Bradford?"

Ryan nodded. "He collapsed. Someone in line called for an ambulance while someone else ran to the police station to get Sheriff Billings. The sheriff is afraid Mr. Bradford was poisoned."

"What made him come to that conclusion?" Scott asked.

"One of the witnesses reported that Mr. Bradford had a seizure before he collapsed," Ryan said. "That's inconsistent with a heart attack."

"But couldn't the seizure have been caused by another medical condition?" Luis spread his hands. "I have an uncle who has epilepsy. He has seizures."

"True. There are lots of reasons, besides being poisoned, that might have caused Mr. Bradford's seizure and subsequent collapse." Ryan shrugged. "But Sheriff Billings has excellent instincts, and he asked that a full toxicology screen be done."

"Does he suspect Aunt Bess?" My voice sounded small and strained, even to my own ears.

"No, but since Mr. Bradford was selling desserts from the café, Sheriff Billings wanted me to see if I can get some samples of what he got here." Ryan lifted one hand as if to bat away the barrage of questions he feared might be volleyed at him. "What Mr. Bradford had left at the food truck has been bagged up for testing. We also found a smaller box he'd taken from here, but it contained only crumbs."

"The sheriff does think we're responsible for—" I gulped. "—for what happened to Mr. Bradford, doesn't he?"

Ryan took both my hands in his. "He doesn't. But he has to be thorough."

"Ryan's right," Scott said. "The Sheriff's Department can't show any signs of favoritism toward the café. And it's possible we could've inadvertently used a tainted ingredient, or Mr. Bradford could have been allergic to something we gave him."

"Exactly." Ryan appeared relieved that Scott was willing to help him explain the Department's position. "You're not currently suspects, but we need to find out exactly what happened to Mr. Bradford and determine if there was anything harmful in the food sold to him this morning."

"None of our other customers reported anything tasting off." I took a mental inventory of the day. "No one got sick while they were here."

"Also, your mom had a cinnamon roll, just like Mr. Bradford did," Luis pointed out.

"That's right." For a few seconds, I wrestled with the decision to call her or not. I didn't want to spoil her day; but if she was feeling ill, I wanted her to get to the hospital immediately. "Excuse me."

I got up and retrieved my phone from my purse, which was behind the counter. Pulling up my contacts, I pressed Mom's number and hoped I could sound normal.

"Hey, sweetie," she said. "What's going on?"

"I just wanted to check and make sure you're having fun."

She laughed. "I'm having a blast. I found the cutest pair of shoes. I can hardly wait for you to see them."

"I'll be looking forward to it. Have you got an outfit in mind to wear them with?"

"I'm still looking for that," she said. "How about I bring something home for dinner so neither of us has to cook or clean up?"

"That would be fantastic, Mom. Thanks."

"Any special requests?"

"Nope. It's your day—you choose."

When I returned to the table, I said, "Mom is blissfully ignorant of everything that's been going on in Winter Garden in her absence. As I imagine you heard, I didn't tell her anything. I figure there will be plenty of time for her to panic with the rest of us when she gets home."

"No need to panic, Amy-girl." Scott patted my arm. "Your mom is fine. As far as we know, so is everyone else who ate here today."

I groaned. "All but one."

Chapter Six

A few minutes and one call from Sheriff Billings to Ryan later, I called Mom back and told her not to bring food home after all.

"Why not?" she asked.

"I want to get a few people together, and I'll order pizzas. Does that sound all right with you?"

"No. That sounds like there's something you're not telling me. Anytime you throw an impromptu dinner party at my house, there's trouble you're trying to figure out how to disentangle from. What's going on?"

Gulping, I said, "It's...you know."

"No, I don't. Tell me."

Since I had the phone on speaker, I looked around the table, hoping one of the men would help me. Luis began examining the ceiling tiles, Ryan shrugged, and Scott frowned.

At last, Scott whispered, "Just spill it."

"The food truck guy died, and Aunt Bess was hiding in his bathroom when it happened."

"What?" Her voice echoed in the nearly empty dining room, and I was glad I wasn't holding the phone to my ear.

"Jenna, it's Ryan. Everything is going to be okay. We're just meeting to hear what Aunt Bess has to say and to see if she might have seen or heard something that will help us determine what happened to Mr. Bradford."

Mom was muttering unintelligible things, so I told her we'd see her soon and ended the call.

"Well, that went better than I'd thought it would," I said.

"It did?" Luis asked.

"I don't know. I might be lying to myself, but that's what I need to believe right now. Mom took the news as well as could be expected, and everything is going to be all right. Great, even. Right?"

Ryan squeezed my hand. "Right."

Taking an order pad and pen from my apron pocket, I asked, "What kind of pizza does everyone want? Luis?"

"Anything is fine with me," he said. "I like all kinds."

"Same here," Scott said. "Mind if I bring Leslie?"

"Of course not." I looked at Ryan. "Ham and pepperoni?"

"You know it. What about Homer? Sausage?"

"Yeah. We know he likes sausage," I said. "If he doesn't like pizza, I'll make him something else. And I think I know everyone else well enough to get their pizza order right. I don't dare ask Jackie anything."

"About that." Luis took a deep breath. "What's been going on with her the past couple of days? She's been in a bad mood and not talking with anybody. She's even been kinda short with the customers."

"It all started with this food truck business." I stood and removed my apron. "She wanted to change up the plan for the week, and Scott and I refused. We'd already spent money on this week's food, and we couldn't simply scrap our plan in order to make the same foods Mr. Bradford was serving. It didn't make sense."

"I get that she felt threatened by the food truck," Scott said. "But there wasn't anything to get all upset about. People go to Abingdon and Brea Ridge every day for breakfast or lunch, and it doesn't hurt our business."

"I'm feeling like the food truck was simply a match in the powder barrel," I said. "She apparently doesn't feel like she's a decision maker in the business, even though I've gone out of my way to give both of you an equal say." I paused. "I have, haven't I?"

"You have," Scott said. "You and Jackie are both overthinkers. You need to chill a little."

Rolling my eyes, I said, "Tell that to Aunt Bess, who hides in the bathroom of a food truck as it's getting towed to police impound."

The guys laughed. I didn't. I had a bad feeling about this whole mess.

I went home to feed Rory and Princess Eloise, and then I took a quick bath. I slipped on a long-sleeved t-shirt and jeans before sitting down at my vanity and putting on makeup. The routine helped me to regroup and steel my nerves for the evening.

Since it was supposed to storm later, Ryan picked me up in his red sports car and drove us to the top of the hill. I was grateful. If I'd had to walk up the driveway to the big house, I might've turned around, ran back to my place, and refused to come back out.

We went in through the side door where Mom was sitting alone at the kitchen table.

Bending to kiss her cheek, I said, "Hi, Mom. I've ordered the pizzas, and they should be arriving soon. Who else is here already?"

"Just Aunt Bess, Jackie, and Homer," she said.

I took a deep breath. "I should go have a word with Jackie alone."

"Jenna, I can set up a drink station, if you'll tell me where everything is," Ryan said.

"I'll help you. I wasn't expecting company, so I don't have a lot—water, iced tea, and white grape juice."

"Would you like me to go to the store and get some more drinks?" he asked.

"No. I'd rather you stay. I might need you to arrest Jackie and Amy if they come to blows."

I pretended I didn't hear Mom's joke as I walked into the living room. Aunt Bess and Homer were happily watching a game show on TV. Jackie was leaning against the door jamb with her arms folded.

Gayle Leeson

After tapping Jackie on the shoulder, I jerked my head toward the porch, indicating that I wanted her to follow me outside. Although I wasn't a hundred percent sure she'd go, I was relieved when she did. I sat on the swing, and Jackie took a seat beside me. I began to move the swing, glad that Jackie hadn't chosen to sit on one of the nearby rockers. By sitting beside me, she wouldn't have to look at me—and vice versa—while we talked.

"Why didn't you tell me where you were going today?" I asked.

"I had it under control."

"Maybe so, but I didn't appreciate having to find out from Ryan that Aunt Bess had been taken in for questioning and that Woodrow Bradford had been poisoned."

Jackie swung her head around to face me. "Bradford was poisoned?"

"The lab hasn't confirmed it yet, but Sheriff Billings is confident that's what happened. I've invited a few people over for pizza so we can all hear Aunt Bess and Homer's version of the story and, hopefully, figure out what we should do."

"I'll invite Roger." Jackie glared at me. "If that's okay with you, I mean."

I didn't rise to the bait. "I think that's an excellent idea."

Finally, we were all sitting around the dining room table: Mom, her boyfriend, Clark, Aunt Bess, Homer, Jackie, Roger, Luis, Scott, Leslie, Ryan, and me. Everyone had slices of pizza; and if anyone was disappointed in the drink selection, no one said so.

"Homer, Aunt Bess, what happened today?" I asked.

"We left the Down South Café at approximately eleven-fifteen a.m.," Homer said.

"Homer drove me to the municipal building where the food truck was parked," Aunt Bess said. "He left me to stake out the truck while he went into the post office to buy some stamps."

"The place was packed—it being lunchtime and all—and while I waited for my turn at the window, I got to talking with Jerry Fremont." Homer sipped his water. "Jerry was mailing out a package to his daughter, who recently had her third baby—Jerry's fifth grandchild—out in Arizona. Jerry is saving up to go out there for a visit. He hopes to get there within the next month."

I clenched my fists in my lap, trying not to show my frustration with his meandering pace.

Homer continued. "Muhammad Ali once said, 'Live every day as if it were your last because some-day you're going to be right.' Jerry knows that too, and he sure does want to see his new grandchild."

"Aunt Bess, what were you doing in the food truck bathroom?" Ryan asked.

"Well, honey, I had to pee." She shrugged. "I asked that Bradford man if I could go in, and he said yes. He was awfully nice. I think now that I might've misjudged him before. I don't believe he was trying to be underhanded toward the café. He was just try-ing to make an honest dollar, you know?"

"Why were you still in the bathroom when the truck was towed away?" I asked her.

"I heard a commotion and was afraid to come out."

"What kind of commotion?" Mom asked.

"Things getting knocked over." Aunt Bess slowly took a bite of pizza and looked around at us inno-cently as she chewed. She was the center of attention and was loving every second of it. She swallowed, dabbed her mouth with her napkin, and said, "I thought maybe he was trashing the truck and was planning to blame it on me. So, I stayed in there because I didn't want my fingerprints to be found anywhere except the bathroom, which I left exactly as I found it. Except when I went in, it was in the municipal parking lot; and when I came out, it was in the impound yard."

"The sounds you heard of things being knocked over might've been when Mr. Bradford suffered his seizure," Clark said.

"Or maybe the man he'd been arguing with before returned," Homer said.

"He was arguing with someone?" Ryan asked. "You witnessed this confrontation?"

"No, not me. It was one of the ladies who works at the post office. She was talking about it to her coworker." Homer put his forearms on the table and leaned in. "Janine came back from lunch, and she was waiting for Cindy to finish up with her customer so Janine could take over and Cindy could go on her break. While she was waiting for the receipt to print out, Cindy asked Janine what she had for lunch. Janine said she had the chicken and waffles from Better'n Yer Mama's. She said the food was good but that she'd had to wait too long to get it because there was a man at the front of the line arguing with the owner. Janine said that man didn't even get any food."

"Was he arguing about the food?" Luis asked.

"I don't know. The receipt was done printing by then, and Cindy handed it to her customer and left. I reckon Janine either didn't think the tale was worth telling, or else she figured it wasn't any of our business."

"Hmph. It was as much the customers' business as it was Cindy's," Aunt Bess said. "And Janine's, for that matter."

"I agree," Homer said.

"I'll go to the post office and talk to Janine about it tomorrow." Aunt Bess raised her glass to her lips.

"I'll take care of it, Aunt Bess," Ryan said. "The weather is supposed to be bad all day tomorrow."

"He's right," I added. "And you know how you hate being out in the rain."

"Makes your hair frizz something awful," Mom said.

Aunt Bess lowered her glass. "Is it supposed to be as bad as all that?"

"Yes, ma'am," Roger said. "I told my men to be prepared to work indoors all day tomorrow and likely the next."

"Well, Ryan, if you're sure you can handle it, I'll leave you to it," Aunt Bess said.

"Clark," Scott said, "what, if any, poison might make a person have a seizure before collapsing?"

"I hate to speculate—after all, there hasn't been a formal ruling of poison or any other cause of death released by the medical examiner yet—but playing devil's advocate, I'd say ethylene glycol."

"Antifreeze," Roger said.

"It's tasteless," Clark said. "Anyone can buy it. And, yes, it could cause someone to have a seizure in the final stages."

"I think it smells like brown sugar, so Mr. Bradford wouldn't have suspected anything even if he'd smelled it," Leslie said.

I wondered how on earth someone could poison Mr. Bradford with antifreeze. Surely, it had to be someone who lived or worked with him.

"But, again, we're jumping the gun," Clark said. "We don't know for certain that Mr. Bradford was poisoned with antifreeze or anything else at this point."

"True," Ryan said. "But Sheriff Billings felt fairly certain. And his hunches are rarely wrong."

Chapter Seven

When I arrived at the café the next morning, I was wearing my rain jacket and carrying my umbrella; but although the clouds looked ominous, it wasn't raining yet. Scott was already there rolling out biscuit dough.

"Good morning," I said, checking the clock over the serving window to make sure I wasn't late.

"Hey, Amy-girl. Woke up early and decided to come on in and get started."

"Thank you. Anything you need to talk about?"

"Not really." He floured a biscuit cutter and began stamping out rounds of dough. "I just hope that if somebody poisoned Mr. Bradford, they didn't use our pastries to do it."

Before I had a chance to respond, Leslie came into the café. "I couldn't sleep last night, so I did a deep dive online to see what I could learn about Woodrow Bradford."

"What did you find out?" Scott asked, transferring the biscuits to a baking sheet.

Leslie took a seat at the counter.

"Would you like some coffee?" I asked.

"Yes. The French vanilla please."

She knew we kept three pots of coffee going throughout the day: French vanilla, dark roast, and decaffeinated. I poured Leslie and me cups of coffee and then asked Scott if he'd like one.

"No, thanks. I'm fine. I had coffee when I first got here." He put the biscuits into the oven and set the timer before joining us at the counter. "Sorry you couldn't sleep either, Les."

Leslie gave him a quick peck on the lips. "It's okay. I'm sure the police have already researched Woodrow Bradford's background, but they could've missed some of these leads."

"We appreciate your help, babe, and I'm sure the police will too," Scott said. "What did you find?"

Taking her phone from the front pocket of her purse, she said, "Mr. Bradford used to be in business with this guy—" She turned her phone around to show us a photo of a man with gray and white streaked hair and dark blue eyes. "His name is Jim Normand, and he owns a restaurant in Brea Ridge called Epic Eats."

"I've heard of that place," I said. "Ryan and I had planned to go there one evening, but then Sarah told us about a whole party of people who got sick there. They're filing suit against the restaurant."

My best friend, Sarah, worked for Billy Hancock, the only attorney with an office in Winter Garden. Mr. Hancock was handling the civil case because he knew the family involved. They'd been celebrating a ninety-second birthday, and—according to the lawsuit—they'd left the restaurant that evening with the worst case of food poisoning any of them had ever had.

"Send me the photo of that Normand guy, and I'll text it along with his name and the restaurant information to Ivy," Scott said. "Maybe he's the one who was arguing with Mr. Bradford yesterday morning."

"That's what I was thinking too." Leslie sent the photo to Scott's phone. "There's something else. When Mr. Bradford posted his first photo of the food truck, a woman commented with some choice words about how he'd stolen her idea. Her name was Helen Madison."

Scott was already texting Ivy. "I'll include that too."

"I'm sure the police will want to talk with her." I smiled. "Your aunt must be so proud of you. You really are following in her footsteps."

Leslie's aunt, Daphne, was a renowned cake decorator and amateur sleuth in Brea Ridge, and she'd helped the police solve more than one tough case. Leslie and Scott had met at one of Daphne's cake decorating masterclasses and had been dating ever since.

Leslie was pulling out of the parking lot when Jackie and Luis walked into the café together.

"Is everything okay?" Luis asked. "It's not like Leslie to come in this early."

"She was apparently up all night worrying about Mr. Bradford's murder." I finished my coffee.

"There's a lot of that going around," Scott said. "At least, Leslie was investigating. In fact, she got a couple of solid leads that I've already passed on to Ivy."

"That's great." Luis hung up his jacket and tied a black apron around his waist.

"Before everybody gets really busy, I'd like to apologize for how upset I got about this food truck business," Jackie said. "I felt as if my opinion didn't count, even though I'm an equal partner in the business now." She held up her hands to keep Scott and me from speaking. "There's no need to say anything or to try to make me feel better. I know you care about me, and I know you did the practical thing by not changing the menu to compete with the food truck."

"Jackie, I—"

She cut off my words with a firm shake of her head "As I told you, there's no need to say anything. Let's get to work."

"I've got a feeling it's gonna be an all-hands-on-deck day today," Scott said.

I had my doubts, since no one really understood what had happened to Mr. Bradford yet—and he'd been reselling Down South Café pastries from his truck—but Scott had made an accurate prediction. We were swamped, and everybody who came in seemed to be buzzing about Mr. Bradford and giving their take on what had happened to him.

I had little time to listen to the scuttlebutt, but I did catch a few phrases here and there.

"Somebody said he'd been in witness protection, but the criminals he was running from found him and did him in."

"I heard he was smuggling drugs out of the food truck."

"The rumor I got wind of was that he was a fugitive and was killed trying to escape the law."

Nothing I heard made any sense, especially those that indicated Mr. Bradford was a criminal. Had he been a criminal, why would he have set up shop in the parking lot of the Sheriff's Department? But I was happy that none of the speculation I overheard involved any wrongdoing on the part of the Down South Café.

Or, at least, that was the case until Helen Madison showed up shortly after twelve o'clock when the café was at its fullest and accused us of poisoning Wood Bradford.

Okay, let me back up.

When Helen Madison walked into the café, she seemed normal. Pleasant even.

"Hi! Welcome to the Down South Café!" Scott's greeting was warm and effusive, as usual.

I believe the crowded dining room had given him—and the rest of us as well—the notion that nobody even remotely blamed us for what had happened to Mr. Bradford. I'd even begun to hope that the man hadn't been poisoned at all, that he'd suffered some medical emergency that mimicked signs of poisoning and had died of natural causes.

"Thank you." The woman we'd later learn was Helen Madison then pulled out a chair. Instead of taking a seat, she stood on it.

"Whoa." Scott hurried toward her. "I don't think that's such a good idea."

"On the contrary, it's an excellent idea." She raised her voice. "May I have everyone's attention please?"

Feeling a jolt of apprehension course through me, I removed a burger from the grill before it burned. When I turned, I met Jackie's eyes. I didn't have a mirror, but I imagined I looked frightened. My cousin looked enraged. She pushed past me into the dining room. I followed her from the kitchen.

"Please, let's get you down from there before you get hurt," Scott said.

He was standing on one side of the woman, and Luis was on the other.

"You'd like that, wouldn't you?" she asked. "To hush me up before I can speak my mind." She turned her attention back to the rapt patrons. "Do you know what you're eating? These people are responsible for the death of Woodrow Bradford, proprietor of the Better'n Yer Mama's food truck."

Jackie didn't adopt Scott and Luis's considerate approach. She stomped to the chair on which the woman stood and said, "You get down off that chair right now, or I'll knock you off it. You're trespassing and slandering the impeccable reputation of this establishment, and I will be pressing charges."

"Good!" the woman cried. "Call the police! See if I care!" Her words were brash, but she did step down from the chair. It was a good decision.

Speaking of good decisions, I surmised that calling the police was an excellent idea, so that's what I did. Well, actually, I texted the police—Ryan—briefly explained the situation and asked him to get here ASAP. By the time he and Sheriff Billings arrived, Helen Madison was still there, but most of our patrons had left.

Ryan took our statements while Sheriff Billings led Helen Madison over to a table to presumably find out if she'd simply lost her ever-loving mind or if she had a logical reason for thinking we had something to do with Wood Bradford's death.

"Are you okay?" Ryan asked me quietly.

I nodded. "She didn't try to harm anyone...other than our business, that is." I walked him through the events as I'd witnessed them.

When Ryan went to speak with Scott, I walked over to the cash register to take care of an older couple who dined at the café on a regular basis.

"It's on the house today," I said. "We're truly sorry that your meal was disturbed."

"Nonsense," the gentleman said. "Our food was delicious, as always, and we wouldn't dream of stiffing you on the bill like some of the other folks who flew out of here like they'd been shot out of a cannon."

"Yeah, and if we didn't feel sorry for y'all as well as for that poor woman, we might've even enjoyed the floor show," his wife said. "But we've seen grief take its toll on a lot of people, so try not to be too hard on her."

I started to insist on giving them their meal for free; but they were right about other customers running out without paying when Helen Madison began hurling her accusations, and I knew we were going to be in the red at the end of the day. And since this was a small town and news traveled fast, I also feared that news of the debacle might keep all but our most faithful patrons away tomorrow too.

Giving my customers a tight smile as they left, I couldn't help but feel a little resentful of their remark not to be too hard on "that poor woman," when "that poor woman" might well have done major damage to the Down South Café.

We typically closed at three o'clock in the afternoon. I looked at the clock and saw that it was only around one-thirty, but I went ahead and began the day's cleanup. I didn't expect anyone else to come in today; and, frankly, when Ryan and Sheriff Billings were through questioning everybody, I wanted to go home and feel sorry for myself.

I'd done nothing but be polite to a rival. Gave him the old "welcome to the neighborhood, let's be friends" spiel. And what had it earned me? The anger of my cousin-slash-business partner and the reputation of the café in shreds.

So, yeah, I already had a head start on the feeling sorry for myself portion of the evening. I just needed to go home, put on some slow jazz, bake something, and cuddle up with Rory.

I was so intent on cleaning the grill that I started when Luis said my name.

"Didn't mean to scare you," he said. "Are we closing early or something?"

"Given all that's happened this afternoon, I feel that would be best. Don't you?"

He shrugged.

"We've got lots of leftover food," I said. "Box up whatever you'd like and take it home to your family."

"Thank you, but—"

"But what?"

"You aren't gonna let the actions of one crazy lady make you give up on the café, are you?"

His words brought tears to my eyes. "No. But today, I need to go home and regroup. These past few days have simply been too much for me, and I need to get away from here for a little while. Does that make sense?"

Nodding, he said, "I can finish the grill if you want to go."

I hugged him, thanked him, gathered my things, and left.

Chapter Eight

As soon as I walked through the door, I hung my jacket and purse on a wooden peg and threw myself onto the sofa. Rory quickly climbed onto my lap and licked my chin. Even Princess Eloise sensed the sad shape I was in and came to lie next to me.

I had myself a good cry, and then I went upstairs and soaked in a warm, lavender-scented bath. The rain plinking against the window further helped to soothe me.

Sufficiently calm but still glum, I dressed in my softest fleece loungewear and went downstairs to flip through my recipe book for the perfect comforting dessert.

Chocolate Caramel Coffee Pretzel Bars—that should do the trick.

The recipe was a bit time-consuming, but I considered that a good thing. Following the steps forced me to concentrate on the process rather than my problems.

While the bars were baking, I went into the fancy room, stretched out on the white chaise, and stared up at the ceiling. I wondered who Helen Madison was to Woodrow Bradford and what had possessed her to make such a scene in the café.

I hopped up and got my laptop. Taking a page from Leslie's book, I logged onto social media to search for answers. There were several Helen Madisons, but it didn't take long to find the one I was looking for—not only did I recognize her in the profile photo, but it had been taken while she was posing on a stepladder. The woman obviously had a thing for heights.

Woodrow Bradford was listed among her friends. I searched for his name within her posts and found some interesting information. The first post in which she'd tagged Mr. Bradford was a link she'd shared from a local television station with a story about Better'n Yer Mama's food truck.

Helen Madison had commented, "Didn't even mention me? I see how it is! LOL"

He hadn't responded.

Why would a news item about Wood Bradford's food truck mention her? I kept scrolling.

About a week before she'd shared the news link, Helen had posted a slightly blurred image of a menu with the caption, "Something exciting is in the works! Can hardly wait to share it with everyone!" The caption was followed by heart, celebration, and food emojis.

Was Helen Madison Mr. Bradford's partner in the food truck? That would explain her "mock" outrage at not being mentioned in the news story. Leslie had said Helen had "a few choice words," but I couldn't find her comments on his post. Had Helen gone back and deleted anything that might've been incriminating?

I went back to the post with the television station's link, clicked, and watched the interview. Mr. Bradford was smiling from ear to ear as he stood beside his food truck. A young female reporter introduced him.

"I'm here with Woodrow Bradford, proprietor of the brand new food truck, Better'n Yer Mama's. Tell

us, Mr. Bradford, how did you come up with the name?"

"Well, I'm a country boy, and I can tell you that nobody's cooking was better than my mama's." He laughed. *"And she taught me everything she knew. So much so that I'm willing to bet that my cooking is better than yer mama's."*

"Aren't you afraid some people might be put off by the name? That they might find it insulting?" the reporter asked.

"Not at all, Julie. It's provocative, I'll grant you that, but it's meant to be taken lightly. I figure folks will either come for good, old-fashioned cooking like their mothers used to make, or they'll come to taste my food and tell me I'm wrong. Either way, I see it as a win."

"I see. This isn't your first foray into the restaurant business, is it, Mr. Bradford?"

Was I imagining it, or did Mr. Bradford's face darken at this question? Either way, he recovered before answering.

"It sure isn't. For the past five years, I was co-owner of Epic Eats, a restaurant in Brea Ridge."

No wonder he'd looked uncomfortable. As a co-owner, Mr. Bradford would surely be named in the food poisoning lawsuit currently pending against

Epic Eats. He certainly wouldn't want potential customers associating his food truck with near-fatal food poisoning. I made a mental note to check to see how Epic Eats was faring these days.

"Why did you decide to make such a drastic change?" Julie asked.

"I wanted to do something less traditional that would allow me to work whatever hours I please, go wherever I want, and cook the foods I enjoy. I'm planning on offering different menu items each day."

"Wow, that sounds like quite an undertaking."

With another laugh, Mr. Bradford said, "I'm calling it a labor of love."

"Where can our viewers expect to find Better'n Yer Mama's in the coming weeks, Mr. Bradford?"

"I plan on starting out in Winter Garden. Seems to me there's an untapped market there."

"Well, we wish you the best. This is Julie Kwon reporting."

I closed my laptop and retrieved my phone.

Sarah answered in her professional voice. "Good afternoon. Billy Hancock's office, Sarah speaking. How may I help you?"

"Hi, Sarah, it's me."

"Amy!" The voice instantly became that of the Sarah I knew. "What's up?"

"Have you heard about Woodrow Bradford?"

"No. Should I have?"

"Probably not. For some reason, I thought his death might have been on the news, but maybe—"

"His death?" she interrupted. "What happened?"

"Sheriff Billings thinks he was poisoned, but the lab results haven't come back yet. This only happened yesterday." I sighed. "Here's the thing, though. He visited the café yesterday morning and bought some desserts to resell from his food truck."

"And?"

"And what if somehow our desserts were used to kill Mr. Bradford?" I asked.

"Oh, Ames, that's ridiculous. You're letting your nerves get the best of you. What you need is a night out."

"Both of those things might be true—the nerves and needing a night out, I mean—but today, a woman named Helen Madison came into the café, stood on a chair, and warned our patrons that they had no idea what they were eating and that she thinks we poisoned Wood Bradford."

She gasped. "I don't even know where to start unpacking what you just told me. Who is this woman? What was she to Bradford? Did Jackie make bail?"

That last question made me laugh. "Jackie didn't thrash her. She threatened to, but she showed considerable restraint. As for who the woman is, I hoped you could help me find out."

"Sure. I'll do whatever I can."

"Mr. Bradford gave an interview about his food truck a couple of weeks ago, and he mentioned he was involved with Epic Eats prior to starting this new venture. Is he named in the food poisoning lawsuit against Epic Eats?"

"Let me look."

I heard keys tapping as she located and opened the file on her computer.

"He isn't," she said. "At the time of the incident, he was no longer a partner with Jim Normand."

"Huh. Is Helen Madison mentioned anywhere in the lawsuit?"

More clicking of keys.

"Nope."

"Refresh my memory on the food served please," I said.

"Epic Eats had been reserved for a large birthday party. Some members of the family were vegan so the chef made a casserole dish using what he thought was chicken of the woods, an edible mushroom that's considered a delicacy among foodies," Sarah said.

"The mushrooms are expensive, which is why the restaurant was foraging for its own. However, this particular batch of chicken of the woods turned out to be jack-o-lantern mushrooms, which are poisonous."

"Did they not realize their mistake before the family filed suit against the restaurant?"

"Actually, they did. When they turned out the lights and got ready to leave the evening after the party, they noticed that the mushrooms were glowing in the dark."

"Is that normal?" I asked.

"It is for jack-o-lantern mushrooms, but not for chicken of the woods. Jim Normand quickly called the woman who had booked the party, but by then, everyone who'd eaten the casserole was sick. Their defense is that the substitution of the mushrooms was an accident and was done without malice aforethought. But between you and me, all the chef had to do was turn off the light to see if the mushrooms were bioluminescent. That's why Billy and I are confident that the plaintiffs will win this case."

"How is Epic Eats doing now?"

"I don't know. Why?" I heard a smile creep into her voice. "You want to go snoop, don't you?"

"Kinda. But I don't want to eat poisonous mushrooms and die like the elephant king in *Babar*."

She laughed. "We'll make sure that whatever we eat has no mushrooms in it. When do you want to go?"

"Could you and John double date with Ryan and me tomorrow evening?"

"I'll check with John and see. And you'd better see if you can talk Ryan into it."

"All right. I'll call you tomorrow," I said.

As I ended the call, the oven timer dinged. I hurried to the kitchen and transferred the bars from the oven to a cooling rack.

There was a brief knock on the front door before Jackie opened the door and called, "It's me!"

"In the kitchen!"

"Smells good," she said, joining me in the kitchen. She pulled out a chair and took a seat. "I came to see if you're all right."

"Honestly, no, I'm not. As a matter of fact, I'm really glad tomorrow is Saturday. I almost wish we could be closed."

"That doesn't sound like the Amy I know. That Amy doesn't run from a fight."

"That's not me," I said. "That's you."

A Recipe for Murder

"No. I run toward fights. You stand your ground and don't run away from them."

I took a seat across from her as Rory came racing to bring her a tennis ball. "Do you regret accepting the partnership?"

"I don't know." She ruffled the fur on Rory's head and then tossed the ball for him to chase. "Owning and operating a café was always your dream, and I'm not a hundred percent sure I'm cut out for it."

"I understand, especially with everything that's happening. We might go belly-up, if Helen Madison has her way. If you want out, just say so, and I'll return your investment."

She stiffened. "Is that what you want?"

"I want what I've always wanted—for you to be happy."

"Thanks. I'll give it some serious consideration, and we'll talk about it again in a few days." She stood. "Who knows? Maybe we'll both feel better when this whole Wood Bradford mess blows over."

"I think you mean *if.*"

Chapter Nine

I had just finished cutting the caramel pretzel bars when Ryan arrived. Both Rory and Princess Eloise made a beeline for him, as usual, but he only had eyes for the pretzel bars.

"Those look great," he said.

"Help yourself. Would you like some coffee or cocoa?"

"I'll take a bottle of water, if you have a cold one." He ate one bar and reached for another.

I grabbed a water from the fridge. "I can whip us up some dinner."

"That'd be great. I didn't get lunch." He took a bite of the second pretzel bar. "These are delicious. Have you made them before?"

"Nope. I came across the recipe this afternoon while I was looking for something to bake." He knew that baking kept my hands busy while my mind was in a tangle.

"Well, that recipe is definitely a keeper."

Taking a bite of one of the slightly sticky bars, I had to agree. "They are good. You should take them home with you."

"I'll take some, but you'd better share with Aunt Bess. If she were to find out you made a new treat and didn't save her any, you and I both might end up on her People I've Outlived board."

I laughed. "Excellent point. So, how about sloppy Joe's for dinner?"

"Fantastic." He went to the sink and washed his hands before finally turning his attention to the impatient pets.

As I began chopping an onion, Ryan casually—which let me know it wasn't casual in the slightest—asked if I'd spoken with Scott.

"No. Why?" I kept my attention focused on the onion.

"After speaking with Helen Madison, Sheriff Billings asked Scott if the café would like to press trespassing charges. Scott said he didn't want to pursue it." He paused. "I thought maybe the two of you had discussed the matter."

"We didn't." I put the chopped onion into a skillet with a little olive oil. "I left. Jackie and Scott had the right to make whatever decision they thought was best."

"Um...Jackie left the café shortly after you did. Scott made the call on his own."

Frowning slightly, I took the ground beef from the refrigerator and began crumbling it into the skillet. "I trust Scott's judgment, and I know that when I go in to work tomorrow morning, he'll tell me why he chose not to press charges and that I'll likely agree with him. But given how angry she was, I'm not sure Jackie will see it that way."

Ryan spread his hands. "Scott was the only partner there, and the sheriff needed an answer. You can tell her that if you think it will help."

Not quite knowing how to respond, I changed the subject. "I talked with Sarah today."

"And how is Sarah?" The lift of his right eyebrow told me he knew I was leading up to something.

"She's fine." I turned my attention to the ground beef, stirring it around with a spatula. "As we were talking, the subject of Epic Eats and the lawsuit against Jim Normand and Woodrow Bradford came up."

"Just happened to come up, did it?"

"All right. I called and asked if Mr. Bradford was a party to the lawsuit, and he wasn't. I thought maybe we could go to Epic Eats tomorrow evening and talk with Mr. Normand to see who he thinks might've wanted to harm his former partner."

"You don't think the sheriff has spoken with Mr. Normand already?" he asked.

"Sure, but—"

"But he's more likely to open up to you and the assistant to the attorney bringing suit against him."

"Ryan, I can't just sit around and do nothing when the reputation of everything I've built is at stake."

He came to stand behind me and slid his arms around my waist. "Okay. We'll go to Epic Eats tomorrow."

Leaning my head back against his chest, I said, "Thank you. It might not help at all, but at least, I'll feel as if I'm doing something."

The next morning at the café, I was telling Scott about the plan to visit Epic Eats that evening.

"Didn't mean to eavesdrop, but did you say you're going to Epic Eats?" Dilly asked, as she and Walter came through the door.

"I did. What do you know? Is it something about the food poisoning incident?" I asked.

"Oh, I heard about that, but I didn't put too much stock in it," she said. "I mean, I'm sure it happened, but it was simply an unfortunate accident. Jim strikes me as a stand-up person."

"You know Mr. Normand?" Scott asked.

"We do," Walter said. "He and I are in the rotary club together."

"Sarah and I are hoping Mr. Normand and/or some of his staff will talk with us about Woodrow Bradford and who might've wanted to harm him." I shrugged. "Have you heard what happened here yesterday?"

"Yes." Dilly patted my arm. "Don't you worry about that woman. No one will take her accusations seriously."

"I don't know. She sure did clear out the dining room yesterday."

Scott looked down at the floor. "I meant to tell you before now, Amy, but Sheriff Billings asked me yesterday if we wanted to press trespassing charges, and I said no. I figured we didn't want any more bad publicity and that it would only make her more sympathetic if I had her arrested."

"Good thinking." I turned back to Dilly. "Do you know Helen Madison?"

Dilly shook her head. "Never heard of her, and I'm sorry for what happened. Why don't Walter and I accompany you and Sarah and your dates to the restaurant this evening? Jim might be more willing to open up to us."

"Thanks," I said. "I appreciate that."

I glanced at the clock. It was nearly time for Homer to come in, and Jackie wasn't back from the Brea Ridge Farmer's Market yet. We took turns on Saturday going to the market for fresh produce and eggs.

Business had been steady so far—a typical Saturday—and I was hopeful that Helen Madison's tirade hadn't done too much damage after all.

With the breakfast rush behind us, I began prepping for the lunch crowd.

"Hey, Amy-girl, we're low on chocolate chip brownies," Scott said, as he breezed into the kitchen. "Do you think I should make another batch?"

Before I could answer his question, Jackie stormed into the kitchen with her cloth tote bags filled to the brim. She dropped the totes onto the floor and clenched and unclenched her fists.

"Did someone cut you off in traffic?" I asked.

"No. This is me calm. This is me after driving from Brea Ridge doing deep-breathing exercises."

"Whoa." Scott held up both hands. "I'm glad I didn't see you when you were angry."

"I take it something happened at the market?" Sure, it was a dumb question, but I felt I had to say something.

"That woman was there—Helen Madison," Jackie said. "She was selling sourdough bread. Just looking at her and remembering what she did to us yesterday infuriated me."

"What did you do?" I asked, dreading the answer. Although, I reasoned, it couldn't be too bad. The police weren't here. Yet.

"I took my fist and smashed three loaves of that bread—that's what I did."

Scott lowered his head, presumably to hide a grin.

"Then she had the nerve to try to make me buy the bread!" Jackie exclaimed. "So I tossed a few bucks on the table and said loudly enough for everyone standing nearby to hear, 'That's for your inconvenience. I'd take the bread, but I'm afraid I'd be poisoned like Woodrow Bradford!'"

"Aunt Bess will be proud," I said.

"Yes, she will," Jackie said.

"Did it make you feel better?" Scott asked.

"Not as much as I'd hoped." She blew out a breath. "I kinda regret it now."

"This might not be the best time to tell you," Scott said, "but when the sheriff asked me if I wanted to press trespassing charges yesterday afternoon, I said no. We still might have time to reconsider, if you want to."

"No, that's all right," she said. "I got my revenge, even though the victory feels really hollow now that my anger has subsided."

"That's usually the way it goes." I patted her shoulder. "Look on the bright side—you can't be arrested for assaulting a loaf of bread."

Chapter Ten

Ryan and I arrived at the restaurant first and waited outside for Sarah, John, Dilly, and Walter.

"How did the partner meeting go this week?" Ryan asked.

"It went fine. Scott and I made sure to get Jackie's input on every decision...to the point where she finally got aggravated and told us to knock it off."

"So, she's getting back to normal then?"

"I believe she is." I told him about the bread incident.

He laughed. "I wish I'd have been there to see that."

"I'm glad I wasn't." I shook my head. "I'd like to know more about Helen Madison's relationship with Woodrow Bradford. Was she his business partner? Romantic partner? Both? Neither?"

"She told Sheriff Billings that they were friends— that's all she'd own up to."

"Brea Ridge has its farmers' market tomorrow afternoon as well, doesn't it?" I asked. "From one until four?"

"Amy—"

"What? I love visiting farmers' markets, you know."

He ran a hand over his face. "After her experience with Jackie, do you honestly think Helen Madison will be happy to see you?"

"No, but I can apologize for Jackie's behavior and, hopefully, get her talking about Mr. Bradford."

"Sweetheart, we're investigating this case and utilizing every resource at the department's disposal."

"I know." I rose up on my tiptoes to give him a quick kiss. "Consider me an additional resource."

Fortunately, Walter and Dilly arrived and effectively ended our discussion. When Sarah and John reached Epic Eats, the six of us went inside. Since we had a reservation, we were immediately escorted to our table.

"Is Jim here this evening?" Walter asked our server, Terry. "I'd love to say hello."

"I'll check," Terry said. "May I take your drinks order?"

We ordered drinks, and after Terry left, Dilly entertained us with a story about Buddy, the raccoon, who'd brought a companion with him to the back porch that evening.

"It seems I'm going to have to provide two biscuits now that Buddy has a girlfriend," she said.

"Just you wait," Sarah said, her dark eyes sparkling. "You'll be feeding an entire family of masked rascals before you know it."

"Baby raccoons!" I clasped my hands together. "Wouldn't they be the cutest things ever?"

"Destructive is what they'd be," John said. "Raccoons can do some serious damage."

The other two men nodded in agreement while we women rolled our eyes. We chose to dwell on the upside—adorable babies—rather than a mob of raccoons wreaking havoc all around Dilly and Walter's house.

We didn't have the opportunity to further debate the positives and negatives of Buddy starting a family because Jim Normand arrived at our table.

"Walter! Good to see you."

The two men shook hands.

"Good to see you, Jim," Walter said. "I heard that your partner died. I'm terribly sorry for your loss."

"Thank you." Mr. Normand glanced away. "We weren't partners anymore, though. Wood had gone out on his own with a food truck."

"I'd heard that but thought he might have kept his interest in Epic Eats as well," Walter said.

"No—only the truck."

Walter nodded. "He'd set up in Winter Garden, hadn't he? Seems he was doing well."

"Yes. His passing is a loss to us all," Mr. Normand said.

"I agree," I said, unable to restrain myself any longer. "I only met Mr. Bradford on a couple of occasions, but he seemed like such a nice person."

"Forgive my lack of manners, Jim. I neglected to introduce you to everyone. You know my lovely wife, Dilly, and these are our friends Amy, Ryan, Sarah, and John."

"Nice to meet you all," Mr. Normand said.

"It's a pleasure to meet you, Mr. Normand." Before I could speak further, Ryan gently gripped my hand under the table.

While I was weighing Ryan's silent warning that this might not be the best time to interrogate Mr. Normand, Dilly spoke.

"Jim, did Mr. Bradford have a girlfriend named Helen Madison?"

"I'm not sure whether or not Wood ever dated Ms. Madison, but she did appear to be obsessed with him. Why do you ask?"

"Well, she went into the Down South Café yesterday, stood on a chair, and accused the staff of being responsible for Mr. Bradford's death," Dilly said.

"Are you kidding?" Mr. Normand asked.

"I wish I were," Dilly said. "It seems Mr. Bradford had bought some pastries from the café on the morning he died, so Ms. Madison jumped to the conclusion that the pastries must have been poisoned."

"That's preposterous." Mr. Normand swayed slightly. "I had no idea Ms. Madison was so disturbed. There's no telling what she's capable of."

"I can only imagine that her grief made her temporarily lose her reason," Dilly said.

"That sort of behavior goes beyond grief. It seems to me that poor Ms. Madison might need some professional help." He inhaled sharply. "I need to alert my staff to be aware of Ms. Madison and to call the police if she comes anywhere near here." He forced a tight smile. "Walter, it was a pleasure seeing you and meeting everyone. I hope you enjoy your dinner, and I appreciate your choosing Epic Eats. Please excuse me." He quickly walked away.

Sarah and I shared a look of silent agreement at being glad we weren't introduced in our professional capacities. Not that it made that much difference, but it might have been awkward for Mr. Normand had he known that she was Billy Hancock's secretary and that I was one of the proprietors of the Down South Café.

"Mr. Normand seemed almost frightened of Helen Madison," Ryan said "I'll have to check with Sheriff Billings to see if he'd got the impression she was dangerous."

"If he had I can't imagine he'd have simply let her go," I said.

"No." Ryan frowned. "He wouldn't have...which leads me to believe Mr. Normand knows something about Ms. Madison that we don't."

After Ryan left that night, I looked out the kitchen window and saw lights on at the big house, specifically, Mom's room. I called her.

"Honey, is anything wrong?"

"No, and I'm sorry for calling so late, but I wanted to have a private conversation with you," I said.

"Don't worry. Big Ears is already sawing logs down the hall."

I laughed. "I know Aunt Bess means well but there are some talks she simply doesn't need to be a part of."

"You're preaching to the choir," she said. "So, what do you need to discuss?"

"Ryan is on duty tomorrow, so he won't be with us for lunch. Do you think Clark would mind if you went with me to drop off a plate to Ryan and then to run a quick—secret—errand?"

"I'm positive Clark won't mind. He's going to be with his daughters tomorrow. That's the thing about dating at my age--you have to accept that the person with whom you're involved had a life before you." Even though she'd told me Aunt Bess was asleep, she still lowered her voice before asking, "What's the errand?"

"I want to go to the Brea Ridge Farmers' Market and talk with Helen Madison."

She groaned. "Hasn't Jackie done enough?"

I wasn't surprised Mom had heard about the smashing of the sourdough. "That's just it. I can use apologizing for Jackie's behavior as an excuse to be there."

"You'd better not let Jackie get wind of that."

"What part of 'secret errand' did you not understand?" I asked. "I'm hoping I can get Helen to talk with me. But if she refuses, you'll be there as my witness that nothing inappropriate happened."

"You think she'd accuse you of slapping her or something?"

"Mom. Yesterday, she accused all of us working at the cafe of poisoning Wood Bradford."

"Good point," she said. "I'll go."

Chapter Eleven

The oven timer dinged as I was frying the breaded butternut squash. Before I could turn around, I heard Mom say, "I've got it. You've got your hands full."

"Thanks," I said.

She put on oven mitts and took the carrot soufflé out of the oven "This smells so good. We haven't had carrot soufflé in ages."

"I don't know why I don't make it more often. It's really simple."

"It does well at the cafe as a side dish too," Jackie said, as she walked into the kitchen. "Maybe we can plan to offer it next week."

Smiling over my shoulder at her, I said, "Maybe so."

"Is it about done?" Aunt Bess called from the living room. "Poor Roger and I are wasting away in here."

"Then come set the table and pour the drinks," I called back. "We aren't serving freeloaders today."

"See how we get done, Aunt Bess?" Roger asked, striding into the kitchen and taking a stack of plates out of the cabinet. "But, then, I guess somebody has to do all the work around here."

"Don't even," Jackie warned. She stirred butter into the mashed potatoes.

"It was a joke, sugar lump," he said.

"I know you didn't just call me a lump." She glared at him.

"You know what I meant." He looked to Aunt Bess for backup, but she was messing around in the refrigerator.

Jackie's glare turned icier.

"You're a sugar...sculpture." He smiled, obviously delighted with his save. "Sweet and beautiful. A true work of art."

"Yeah, yeah. Now you're milking it." She tried but failed to hide her grin. "Go set the table."

I barely stifled a giggle as Roger did as he was told.

"What do you want me to do?" Aunt Bess asked, closing the refrigerator door.

"You can help Roger by putting out the silverware and napkins," Jackie said. "I'll pour the drinks while Aunt Jenna carves the ham."

"It all looks and smells good." Aunt Bess fished forks, knives, and spoons out of the silverware drawer. "What's for dessert?"

"Coconut cream pie or cherry cobbler," I said. "We have both."

"Then I'll have some of both." She paused. "Do we have vanilla ice cream to go with the cobbler?"

"We do," Mom said.

"Good. That'll save Roger from having to go get some."

Mom, Jackie, and I tidied the kitchen while Roger bagged up the trash and Aunt Bess packed up the leftovers for Ryan and anyone else working at the Sheriff's Office today.

Putting the containers in my insulated picnic basket, I asked in the most nonchalant voice I could manage, "Mom, would you like to go with me to drop off these leftovers?"

"I would," Aunt Bess piped up before Mom could answer. "I'm eager to find out if they're making any progress on that Bradford case. That woman who came into the cafe and cut such a shine is awfully suspicious if you ask me."

I widened my eyes at Mom, who didn't appear to be half as concerned as I was. Had she forgotten the plan? We were dropping off the food and then going straight to the farmers' market. I looked at the clock. We were pressed for time already without having to let Aunt Bess interrogate everyone at the police station and then bring her back home only to come up with a plausible excuse to leave again. No way was I taking Aunt Bess to the farmers' market.

"While we're out, we need to run by the Brea Ridge nursing home, Amy," Mom said. "Mother's friend Mildred is there, and I've been promising I'll bring you by." She smiled. "Since Aunt Bess is going, we can make two teams and play gin rummy, if Mildred is feeling up to It."

"That's a great idea," I said. "I haven't seen Mildred for so long."

Aunt Bess grabbed the back of the chair she was standing beside. "Whew! All of a sudden, I'm feeling a little swimmy-headed. I reckon you two had better go on without me."

"Aunt Bess, are you okay?" I asked.

"Yes, I'll be fine," she said. "I don't think I'm up to going out just yet, though. I can wait and talk with Ryan or Sheriff Billings tomorrow."

"I'll stick around and keep an eye on her," Jackie said.

"All right," Mom said, sweeping the picnic basket off the table and heading for the door. "We'll tell Mildred you said hello."

"How did you know that would work?" I asked after we got into the car.

"Aunt Bess despises the nursing home. She says they're for old people." She grinned. "Mildred is a year younger than Aunt Bess."

Laughing, I said, "Way to go. I didn't know how in the world we were going to keep her from going with us to the farmers' market."

"Well, the downside is that now we have to go see Mildred. Otherwise, we're liars."

We didn't make a beeline for Helen Madison's stall. Instead, Mom and I took our time and enjoyed browsing at the farmers' market. Keeping in mind that Jackie had already bought the supplies we needed for the cafe, I concentrated on replenishing my own pantry. I bought blueberry jelly made by a charming older couple who grew their own berries, a pint of strawberries, and some fresh basil.

Mom bought a watermelon and a cantaloupe but made me promise to keep them for her so she wouldn't have to explain to Aunt Bess where the fruit had come from.

"I'll cut them up for you," I said.

"Deal."

The watermelon was too heavy for her to carry around for long, so I offered to take it to the car. She didn't need convincing.

I lugged her tote and mine to the car and placed our purchases on the back seat. When I returned, Mom was standing at Helen Madison's stall. They were chatting amiably.

"Hi," I said, joining Mom at the stall.

Helen didn't realize we were together. She tried to ignore me as she resumed talking with Mom.

"I enjoy working with breads," she said. "I especially like experimenting with different add-ins to see what end result I get. Like this toasted coconut pecan bread."

Butting in, I said, "I apologize for my cousin-slash-partner damaging some of your bread yesterday. She told me she paid you for it."

"Right. No problem." She narrowed her eyes at me. "If you'll excuse me, I'm with a customer at the moment."

"The customer is my mom. She's fine with the interruption."

Helen's accusing stare slid from me to Mom and back again. "Look, I realize I was out of line on Friday, but you people need to either stop harassing me or file trespassing charges against me."

"I don't want to bother you or have you arrested." I lowered my voice. "I simply want to know why you barged into our cafe and accused us of poisoning Mr. Bradford."

Taking a deep breath, she said, "I lost it, okay? I was told that Wood was poisoned. Then I found out he was selling pastries from your cafe."

"That's awfully flimsy evidence for accusing my daughter and her partners of any wrongdoing," Mom said.

"I know. But there's two things for sure about Wood—he couldn't bake to save his life, and he'd never offer something from another vendor without tasting it first."

"You're right," I said. "Mr. Bradford did sample the baked goods before buying them, but we certainly didn't tamper with them. I'm confident the toxicology report will prove that to you."

She rubbed her forehead. "I just don't know how this could've happened."

We were briefly interrupted by a customer who bought a loaf of Helen's bread. Mom and I attempted to appear as nothing more than a couple of shoppers. From the wary glances coming our way, I'm not sure Helen's customers bought our act.

When the woman left, I said, "I don't want to interrupt your business here." Yes, I did realize the irony of that statement as soon as it left my mouth. "Could we buy you a coffee and talk after the farmers' market closes?"

Helen shook her head. "I don't think so."

Mom scoffed. "You don't think so? After what you did to my daughter at her place of business, she still comes here and offers you a kindness, and you don't think so? Fine. We'll stop by the Sheriff's Office on our way back home and take out a warrant for your arrest. Come on, Amy."

We turned to go.

"Wait!" Helen sighed. "There's a coffee shop about three miles from here."

"We passed it on our way here," I said.

"I'll meet you there at four-thirty." Helen's face was still flushed with animosity, but it was apparent she had no desire to be arrested.

I nodded. "We'll be there."

"If you aren't, we will be swearing out that warrant before the end of the day," Mom said.

We were subjected to some curious glances as we made our way back to the car. I could only imagine how those same people must have been looking at Helen Madison.

"Well, we can fill the wait by visiting Mildred," Mom said, as she buckled her seat belt.

"Sounds good." I reached over and squeezed her arm. "Thanks for the backup."

"The insolence of that woman made me see red."

"Being at the farmers' market always reminds me of the one we held in the cafe's parking lot that fall." I pulled out of the spot and onto the highway. "What do you think—should we bring it back this fall?"

"That's something to discuss with your partners, but if I had a vote, it would be no. You've got enough to concern yourself with over the coming months with your wedding, how the cafe will run while you're on your honeymoon, and dealing with Michelle."

"That's true. Thank you for keeping me grounded." I took the turn indicated by the GPS. "My future mother-in-law hasn't been so bad lately."

Mom snorted.

"She hasn't." I laughed. "Okay, she did ask us to invite a bunch of her friends that not even Ryan knows, but he explained that we're trying to keep the ceremony simple."

"Uh-huh. Good luck with that."

"At this point, I'll be happy if Aunt Bess doesn't show up wearing a wedding gown."

"Good luck with that too," Mom said.

Chapter Twelve

We arrived at the retirement home, and Mom took the cantaloupe from the back seat.

"You're taking Mildred a cantaloupe?" I asked.

"Yes. I always bring her a little something when I visit, and I'd intended to get her a treat at the farmers' market. But I got sidetracked, and Mildred enjoys melon, so there you go."

"Works for me. Surely, someone on the kitchen staff won't mind cutting it up for her.

The front desk receptionist happily took the cantaloupe and said she'd have it prepared while Mom and I visited Mildred in her room.

Gayle Leeson

Mom and I softly walked down the antiseptic-smelling hallway to Mildred's room where we found the petite woman perched on a recliner. She was wearing a dress, stockings, a scarf, and black patent pumps as she watched a game show from the 1980s on television.

"Hello, Mildred," Mom said. "You look lovely."

Mildred turned. "Thank you, dear. I went to church this morning and am going to the five o'clock service too." She pushed her glasses up on her nose. "You're more than welcome to join me."

"We would, but we have an appointment at four-thirty." Mom took a seat on one of the two ladder back chairs, and I sat on the other.

"You'll have an appointment with Heaven one of these days, and you'd better be ready for It."

"Yes, ma'am, I know." Mom gestured toward me. "Do you remember my daughter, Amy?"

Mildred switched off the TV. "I do. Knew that must be her the minute you brought her in. She looks just like you."

I wasn't sure about that, but I wasn't about to debate the matter with Mildred. "It's nice to see you again."

"Good seeing you," Mildred said. "What appointment have y'all got that's more important than church?"

"I wouldn't say it's more important than church by any means," I began, looking to Mom for help.

"Me either." Mildred smoothed the skirt of her dress.

"We're meeting with a woman who might be able to tell us who poisoned Woodrow Bradford," Mom said. "Or, at least, tell us who might've wanted to harm the man."

I widened my eyes at Mom. She shrugged. Mildred proceeded as if we were discussing something as trivial as the game show she'd been watching.

"I enjoy a good murder mystery." She reached over to the table beside the recliner to retrieve a pen and a notepad. "Give me the particulars of the case."

Figuring it couldn't do any harm, I took a deep breath and told Mildred about the food truck, meeting Mr. Bradford, his buying pastries from the cafe, his being poisoned, and Helen Madison making a spectacle at the cafe. The only part I left out was Aunt Bess hiding in the food truck bathroom because I didn't really believe that detail was important to the overall narrative.

"Well, there you go," Mildred said, when I'd finished relaying the events. "It's always the first hen to cackle that laid the egg."

"You think Helen Madison made a stink at the cafe because she's the one who poisoned Wood Bradford?" I asked.

"Of course." As if satisfied that she'd tidily solved the case, Mildred returned her notepad and pen to the table. "Wouldn't you try to blame someone else if you'd done the deed? The woman saw your pastries as the perfect patsy."

A young woman wearing scrubs knocked lightly on the open door before entering the room. She was carrying a small white bowl. "Mildred, these ladies brought you a cantaloupe. I've cubed some for you, and the rest is in the fridge. All you have to do is ask for it." She handed Mildred the bowl.

"Oh, boy! I love cantaloupe." Mildred took the bowl and then raised her eyebrows at us. "Hope it's not poisoned."

"What?" The young woman looked alarmed and confused as she reached to take back the bowl.

Mildred pulled the bowl closer. "I was joking, Ruthie. I only said it because we were discussing that poor Woodrow Bradford getting poisoned by his floozy of a girlfriend."

"We don't know that for sure," I said. "I mean about the girlfriend—floozy—whatever..."

Ruthie leaned against the wall. "Is Mr. Bradford going to be all right?"

"No," Mom said quietly. "I'm sorry. Did you know him?"

"Not well, but my mom did," Ruthie said. "She worked with him at Epic Eats. When did this happen? I'm here most of the time, and we advise residents to avoid watching any news programs because it upsets them."

"It happened on Thursday," I said.

"I'm telling you it was that floozy, Helen Madison, who did him in." Mildred popped a melon cube into her mouth.

I silently prayed Ruthie's last name wasn't Madison. "Do you know Helen Madison, Ruthie?"

She shook her head. "No, but Mom might. I need to go call her. She hasn't said anything to me about Mr. Bradford dying, so I'm guessing she doesn't know either. Excuse me." She hurried from the room.

Mildred offered Mom and me the bowl. "Cantaloupe? It's awfully good."

We both politely declined.

As Mom and I were walking down the corridor toward the door, we spotted Ruthie at the nurse's desk.

"Thank you for bringing the cantaloupe in for Mildred," Mom said. "She really enjoyed it."

"It was my pleasure. I told my mom about Mr. Bradford. Turns out, she already knew about his death. She's sad about it. He was always good to her."

"I realize my timing couldn't be worse," I said, "but would your mom be willing to speak with us? Maybe over dinner this evening?"

Ruthie glanced at her watch. "I get off work at seven. She and I could meet you at the burger place near the mall."

"That would be great," I said. "Thank you so much."

We exchanged phone numbers before Mom and I left so Ruthie could get in touch with us if her mom had already made other plans.

"I hope you don't mind my inviting Ruthie and her mother to dinner," I told Mom, as we walked to the car. "I can take you back home after we talk with Helen Madison if you'd prefer."

"Are you kidding? I'm beginning to understand why Aunt Bess enjoys this sort of thing." She smiled. "Besides, by seven o'clock, I'll be more than ready for a burger."

I was surprised to find Helen Madison waiting for us when we arrived at the coffee shop. I'd half expected her to stand us up. She must've thought Mom would make good on her threat to have her arrested for trespassing had she not been here. Come to think of it, she very well might have—I wasn't sure she could, since it was my business, but Helen didn't know that.

Mom and I sat down in the booth across from Helen.

Before giving either of us a chance to speak, Helen asked, "What is it you want to know?"

Her tone put me on the offensive. "Did you poison Wood Bradford and make that ridiculous scene at my cafe to shift blame elsewhere?"

"Of course not!"

I hadn't really expected her to confess, although it would've been nice.

"Then why did you show yourself like that?" Mom asked.

"I don't know." Helen raised a trembling hand to her forehead. "I'd seen Wood earlier that day and knew he was selling some of your pastries, and then I heard he'd been poisoned."

"And what?" I asked. "You thought we'd whipped up a batch of poison cinnamon rolls to serve to all of our customers—including my mom—and your boyfriend just happened to drop in on the wrong day?"

"No. Otherwise, people would've been dying right and left, wouldn't they?" Helen sighed. "But I thought maybe you'd slipped something into the pastries Wood tested. Not necessarily to kill him, but to put him out of commission for a day or two."

"Why would we do that?" While I was more than ready to mount a defense to her accusation, I wanted to hear what she thought our motive might be.

"Everybody knows you had no competition in Winter Garden before Wood came along. At least, not for breakfast."

Mom stood. "I'm going to get some water."

As Mom walked away from the booth, I said, "The day I first learned there was a food truck in Winter

Garden, I went and introduced myself to Mr. Bradford. I welcomed him to the neighborhood."

"Well, aren't you a saint?"

"No, I'm not a saint, but the day my cafe and our food can't stand up to a little competition is the day I fold up my apron and quit."

Mom returned with three bottles of water and handed two of them to Helen and me before she sat back down. "Helen, you know now, even if you didn't know then, that your accusation was false. Who do you know who might've truly wanted to harm Wood Bradford?"

"No one. He was the nicest guy in the world." Helen took the lid off the water bottle and looked at Mom. "Thank you."

"But wasn't he supposed to have included you in his food truck venture?" I asked.

Helen's eyes widened. "Who told you that?"

"You did. On social media."

"Oh...I...I was only joking." She sipped her water. "I mean, he and I had discussed it, but it didn't go any farther than that. Obviously."

At the risk of sounding like Helen's therapist, I asked, "And how did that make you feel?"

"I was disappointed that he didn't bring me on as his partner, but he explained that the food truck was a one-person operation until he could get the business off the ground." She pulled a napkin from the dispenser on the table and dabbed her eyes. "He said maybe he could bring me on board to operate a second truck if the first one was successful."

"Was Wood your boyfriend?" Mom asked.

Helen shook her head. "N-no. We were friends."

"Did the two of you work together at Epic Eats?" I took a drink of water.

"Yeah. I used to work there part-time."

That revelation opened the door to a barrage of questions. I simply had to decide which one to ask first. "What do you think of Jim Normand?"

"He's okay, I guess. He's fair."

"Why did Mr. Bradford leave Epic Eats to go out on his own?" I asked.

"Wood wanted to do his own thing, I guess." She looked at her watch.

If Helen was trying to hint to us that she wanted to leave, she had seriously overestimated the value Mom and I placed on her desires. Or as Nana would've put it, we felt Helen was old enough for her wants not to hurt her.

"Did Wood and Mr. Normand not get along?" Mom asked.

Helen blew out a breath. "They were partners. Did they disagree sometimes? Sure. Did they get along? For the most part, I reckon they did. Now, I'd like to go home if y'all are done giving me the third degree."

"We're not," I said. "Were you working at Epic Eats the night guests got food poisoning from eating jack-o-lantern mushrooms?"

"Yes, but I wasn't involved in the food prep. I'm a server, that's all." She glared at me and then at Mom. "I'm tired, I'm done answering questions, and I'm going home. If that doesn't suit you, then go ahead and have me arrested."

"We're done." I raised my chin. "For now."

Chapter Thirteen

Mom and I met Ruthie and her mom, Brooke, at the hamburger place Ruthie had suggested. We sat with them at the table and made small talk at first—introductions, condolences on the death of Woodrow Bradford, the fact that we were all hungry.

The waitress welcomed us to the restaurant and then asked what we'd like to eat. "I know we're the Burger Boss, but we also have hot dogs, a bunch of great sandwiches, and some yummy desserts."

Ruthie and her mom opted for chili cheese dogs and tater tots. Mom and I ordered the traditional burgers and fries.

We waited until after the waitress had brought our drinks before diving into more serious conversation.

"Brooke, do you enjoy working at Epic Eats?" I asked.

"I did. At first." She avoided looking at me and concentrated on putting her straw into her glass. "I'm not there anymore."

Leaning forward, I asked, "Why did you leave?"

She shrugged. "Everything fell apart when Wood left. I mean it was going downhill before he left; but afterward, it got really bad."

"In what way?" Mom asked.

"Jim became short-tempered with everybody. I believe the business was losing money because he started cutting corners everywhere." Brooke sipped her soda. "He didn't schedule enough people to work a shift, so we were always overworked and stressed out. We stopped using our normal vendors in favor of those with cheaper ingredients. Well, for a while anyway."

"Did Mr. Normand go back to his original vendors after the food poisoning incident?" I asked.

Brooke gave Ruthie a pointed stare.

I rushed to Ruthie's defense. "Ruthie didn't mention anything about it. I have a friend who works in the legal field."

Hopefully, the term "legal field" was vague enough to protect Sarah, although I imagined the case either was or soon would be a matter of public record.

"That snafu never should have happened," Brooke said. "I'd warned and warned Jim not to buy mushrooms from Janine's boys. And I wasn't the only one. Wood had spoken with him about It too."

The waitress brought our food, and for a few minutes, the discussion about Epic Eats and the food poisoning incident were forgotten. It was Mom who returned to the subject of the tainted mushrooms.

"You mentioned Janine and her boys? Do they have a farm or something?"

"Janine works at the post office there in Winter Garden, but her family does live out in the country," Brooke said. "Rather than use our former supplier, Jim had the Harris boys go to the woods and forage for the mushrooms he wanted. It's a wonder no one was killed."

"They very well might have been if you hadn't been there," Ruthie said.

"I only wish I'd caught the mistake before all those people got sick."

"I asked Helen Madison about the mushrooms, but she claimed she never spent any time in food prep." I ate a fry and watched as Brooke stiffened at the mention of Helen's name.

"How do you know Helen Madison?" Brooke's voice was icy.

"She barged into my cafe on Friday, stood on a chair, and announced to our customers that we'd poisoned Wood Bradford."

Ruthie's jaw dropped, and Brooke gasped.

"All but two of our patrons left without paying," I continued. "Not that I can blame them, I guess; but when I found out that Helen had a booth at the farmers' market, Mom and I came to Brea Ridge to confront her and get some answers."

"What was Helen Madison to Wood Bradford?" Mom asked, as she cut her burger in half. "She told us they were friends, but I sensed she'd have liked for their relationship to have been something more."

"Helen chased after Wood for over a year," Brooke said. "She was more of a stalker to him than anything. He got to where he wouldn't even come to work when she was scheduled to be there. He'd swap shifts with Jim to avoid her."

"Huh." I looked at Mom. "And she told us he was going to bring her on as a partner in his food truck business after he got it off the ground." I turned back to Brooke. "Was Mr. Bradford the sort of man who'd say something like that to avoid hurting Helen's feelings?"

She shook her head. "He might've said something like that to anyone other than Helen, but he'd never have given her any encouragement whatsoever. She's the personification of the old saying, 'give an inch, and she'll take a yard.' He knew better."

Mom frowned. "Why would she tell us that then?"

"You've met her." Brooke scoffed. "She's nuts."

"Thank you for coming with me today," I told Mom as we headed home. "I'm sorry it turned into such a long, drawn-out affair."

"I'm not. I enjoyed spending the day with you." She reached over and patted my arm. "We should do this more often."

"Investigate murders? Aunt Bess wouldn't let us see a minute's peace."

"Because she allows us to have so much peace as it is." She laughed. "And you know what I meant. I hadn't realized how much I've missed our one-on-one time together."

"Me too." I slowed down, hoping the car behind us would go ahead and pass. The driver was using the vehicle's high beams and blinding me.

"Something wrong?" Mom asked.

"I just wish this driver would get out from behind us."

Despite my slowing to at least ten miles per hour below the speed limit, the car didn't pass. Nor did the headlights dim.

I sped back up. "I'm going to take a different route. For some reason, I really don't like having this person behind me."

"Do you think your bad feeling could have anything to do with the fact that we interviewed murder suspects all day?"

"Are Mildred, Ruthie, and Brooke murder suspects now?" I asked.

"Mildred and Ruthie, not so much. But I'm not sure I'd rule out Brooke."

"Why's that?" I wondered if I'd missed something.

"Well, she did appear to be pretty chummy with Wood Bradford. I'm not saying she did or said anything suspicious, but there could be more information to mine there than what we uncovered on the surface."

"Good point. I'll mention her to Ryan."

I turned right to get away from the car that was not only blinding me but was now following too close.

The car also took the turn.

"I'm heading for the Winter Garden Sheriff's Office."

Mom twisted around to peer out the back window. "Shouldn't we call the Brea Ridge Police or go to their station?"

"Not yet. I don't want to look foolish if the person is simply oblivious and trying to get home." My eyes flicked to the mirror again. "But if I begin to feel like we're in danger, I'll call."

"I'll look up their number on my phone," Mom said. "That way, I'll be ready."

"Okay. But who'd be following us?"

"At the risk of sounding like Aunt Bess, you never know these days." The light from her phone illuminated the interior of the car.

I made two more turns to get us back onto the main road leading from Brea Ridge to Winter Garden. The vehicle behind me did the same.

Gayle Leeson

Concerned that I'd already frightened Mom, I tried to appear nonchalant. "Have you got any big plans for tomorrow?"

"No, just a typical Monday," she said. "I have the non-emergency number for the Brea Ridge police department pulled up. Do I need to call?"

"I don't think that's necessary yet."

"Is that same car still behind us?"

"It is, but it might be a coincidence that it's following us."

"Amy, you've taken three weird turns to end up on the same road we started out on. If that car is still with us, then it's because it's following us on purpose."

"Probably, but the driver hasn't exhibited any truly threatening behavior. Let's drive to the Winter Garden Sheriff's Office and have Ryan meet us there."

We drove halfway to the police station before the car turned off.

"They're gone now," I said.

"Are you sure?" Mom looked through the side mirror before looking out the back window. "Do you think they're gone for good?"

"I hope so, but I'm not taking any chances. I'm still driving to the Sheriff's Office."

Chapter Fourteen

Ryan was standing beside his police cruiser in the Down South Cafe parking lot when I arrived at work the next morning. I parked my yellow Beetle, got out, and hugged him.

"Thank you for being here, although I still wish you hadn't woken up so early on my account."

"Who says it's on your account? Maybe I'm just trying to wrangle a free breakfast out of you."

Giving him a quick kiss, I said, "You've got it."

"Nothing weird happened last night after I left?" he asked.

Gayle Leeson

"Princess Eloise climbed into my lap for chin scratches, but other than that, no."

"And you weren't followed from your house?"

I unlocked the door to the cafe. "Nope." I flipped on the lights. "Now that I've had more time to think it all through, I could have been blowing the whole incident out of proportion last night."

"You don't blow things out of proportion, and neither does Jenna."

I began readying the three coffee pots, starting with the French vanilla. "Did you find out anything about Janine Harris or her sons and their mushroom business?" I'd filled Ryan in on what I'd learned about Janine from Brooke last night.

"That's a lame attempt to change the subject." He took a seat at the counter. "I haven't even been to the station yet. I'm planning to speak with Mr. Normand to see if Epic Eats did buy mushrooms from the Harrises. If so, I'd like his impression on how Mr. Bradford felt about the boys and vice versa." He spread his hands. "Right now, there's no reason to believe the food poisoning incident and Mr. Bradford's death are connected. Bradford died from ethylene glycol poisoning, not from poisoned mushrooms."

"That's true." I placed a cup of coffee in front of Ryan and then poured a cup for myself. "What would you like for breakfast?"

"A couple of eggs over easy and some whole wheat toast would be great."

"Bacon?" I asked.

He grinned. "I wouldn't turn It down."

"Be back in a jiffy."

I heard Scott come in and greet Ryan as I walked into the kitchen. The men were speaking in hushed tones as I put the bacon on the griddle.

"Good morning," Scott said, as he strolled into the kitchen.

"So, I'm guessing Ryan told you that Mom and I were followed when we left Brea Ridge last night?"

"Yeah. You okay?"

"Sure, I'm fine. Whoever it was didn't follow us all that far." I shrugged. "Just far enough to let us know we were being followed."

Scott took the canister of flour off the shelf and placed it next to the mixing bowl. "Who do you think it was?"

"I don't know. Who does Ryan think it was?"

"He doesn't know either, but he asked me to text him immediately if that Helen Madison chick comes back here."

I handed him the jug of buttermilk before taking two eggs from the fridge. "I don't think she'll ever bother us again. But if she does, you won't have to text Ryan because I'll beat you to it."

It wasn't until after the breakfast rush that Jackie finally got around to asking me about yesterday evening. I was surprised it had taken her that long.

"Why were you and Aunt Jenna out so late?"

"You were still at the big house when I dropped Mom off." I handed her a potato to peel, figuring we might as well work while we talked. "Didn't she tell you where we'd been?"

She got a paring knife and began cutting off the potato peel in a circular motion. It was always an unspoken challenge between us to see who could get the longest peel.

"Aunt Jenna said you visited Mildred and then stopped for food," Jackie said.

"We did." I mentally sized up her potato. It was slightly smaller than mine, and I had an excellent chance of winning this round as long as I didn't accidentally cut the peel.

"I got the feeling there was more to it than Aunt Jenna was saying, that there was maybe something she didn't want to mention in front of Granny."

I weighed my options: tell Jackie the truth and risk making her angry that we went to see Helen Madison; or say nothing and risk making her angry when she discovered the truth, which she inevitably would.

So I told her everything. And, surprisingly, she wasn't angry.

"Who do you think was following you?" she asked. "Helen?"

"Maybe. That's who Ryan believes it was." I placed the peeled potato in the bowl on the counter and held up my peel for Jackie to admire. "Plus, Brooke did refer to Helen as a stalker."

"I wouldn't put anything past Helen after the way she acted on Friday, but I wouldn't blindly trust Brooke or her daughter either if I were you." She added her potato to the bowl and chose another. "I'll beat you this time."

"We'll see about that." I, too, began peeling another potato. "I don't see any reason not to trust Brooke and Ruthie."

"For one thing, their names should be reversed, don't you think? Brooke should be the daughter and Ruthie the mom."

"And that's why I shouldn't trust them?" I asked.

"No. You shouldn't trust them because there's no clear suspect in Wood Bradford's murder yet. It could be anyone."

I paused my knife just long enough to make a mistake and cause the slice of peeling to fall to the counter. "Rats."

Jackie laughed. "Told you I'd beat you."

"Fine." I resumed work on the potato. "But why would Brooke be so forthcoming If she was guilty? I didn't know anything about her or her relationship with Wood Bradford and Jim Normand until Ruthie mentioned it. Brooke could've made up an excuse to avoid having dinner with us."

"She might've thought that would make her look suspicious, so she decided to go ahead with dinner and use that opportunity to point the finger at other suspects."

"That's an excellent point. Still, without Brooke, I wouldn't have learned about Janine from the post office possibly supplying toxic mushrooms to Epic Eats." I heard the bell over the front door jingle and glanced at the clock. "Right on time."

I wiped my hands on a towel and went out to greet Homer. "Good morning, Homer. Who's your hero today?"

"Today, my hero is the English poet, Alexander Pope, who famously said that to err is human and to forgive divine."

"That's too cool, Guru Guy!" Scott gave Homer a high five. "I never knew where that saying came from."

"Oh, he had a lot of good quotes." Homer was thrilled with his rapt audience. "He coined the phrase, 'Fools rush in where angels fear to tread.'"

"Dude! I thought that was Elvis!"

Thankfully, a couple of students came in then and drew Scott back to work.

Setting a cup of coffee in front of Homer, I asked, "How well do you know Janine from the post office?"

"Fair to middling, I reckon. We know each other well enough to say hello if we pass on the street."

"Do you know any of the rest of her family, Homer?"

He squinted at me. "What's this about?"

"I learned yesterday that Janine's sons might've provided mushrooms to Epic Eats," I said.

"You know, Alexander Pope once said that a little learning is a dangerous thing and to drink deep or taste not the Pierian spring."

I frowned. "What's the Pierian spring?"

"It's a mythical fountain of Macedonia that was believed to grant wisdom and inspiration." He emptied a packet of sugar into his coffee.

"What does that have to do with whether or not Janine's sons provided mushrooms to Epic Eats?"

"I have no idea," he said. "I suggest you go by the post office and ask Janine yourself."

Chapter Fifteen

After work, I drove straight to the post office to speak with Janine. Luckily for me, she was working the front desk, and there was no one else in line behind me.

Nodding toward her name badge, I asked, "You're Janine Harris, aren't you?"

She stiffened and raised her chin. "Yes. What's it to you?"

"Brooke from Epic Eats mentioned that you might be able to supply me with some morels. I'm Amy from the Down South Cafe."

Janine relaxed. "What kind are you looking for?"

"Black." I paused. "I heard about the fiasco Epic Eats had with some of their mushrooms. Those weren't procured from you, were they?"

"No." She glanced around to make sure we were still alone. "I have no idea who foraged those mushrooms for Jim Normand. Whoever it was must've been inexperienced and made a mistake, but the chef at Epic Eats should have caught it."

"Right. Morels are easily confused with false morels, so I simply wanted your assurance that I'll be getting what I pay for."

"You have my word. I'll even show you my license if you'd like to see it," she said. "How much would you like?"

"Two pounds to start with. I want to see how they go over with my patrons."

She gave me a nod, wrote an address and amount on a slip of paper, and slid the note across the counter. "I'll be there after five o'clock today."

"All right." I smiled. "See you this evening."

"Keep this between us." Her face was stony as she spoke.

My smile faded. "Of course." Not, I added to myself.

I got into my car and checked the clock on the dashboard. There was plenty of time to get to Brea

Ridge to talk with Jim Normand and make it back to Winter Garden in time to buy the morels. I backed out of the parking space and headed toward Brea Ridge, fingers crossed that Jim Normand was at Epic Eats, that he would talk with me, and that Ryan wouldn't be terribly upset with me for investigating on my own. Again.

There were few cars in the Epic Eats parking lot, and I once again hoped I hadn't wasted the drive. I knew I should've called first, but I was hoping to catch Mr. Normand off guard. I figured he was more apt to tell the truth if he didn't have time to prepare for my questions.

I parked, shouldered my purse, and stepped inside the restaurant.

"Welcome to Epic Eats," a fresh-faced hostess greeted me. "How many will be in your party?"

"It's only me, and I'd like to have a word with Mr. Normand, if he's available."

"May I tell him your name?"

"Amy Flowers. We met Saturday evening."

"Oh." She smiled as if she, Mr. Normand, and I were sharing a secret. I felt my skin crawl. "Have a seat at the bar, and I'll let Jim know you're here."

"Thanks." I took a seat on the first stool and wondered if I'd made a mistake in coming here. Why would the hostess seem to think I'd dropped in because I was interested in Mr. Normand? Did a lot of women come to Epic Eats to throw themselves at its proprietor? Was Mr. Normand known to be a womanizer?

"Amy, dear!"

I started at the sound of my name booming through the restaurant.

Mr. Normand chuckled. "Sorry. I didn't intend to startle you."

"No, I'm sorry," I said. "I was lost in thought."

"Good ones, I hope." He sat on the stool next to mine and motioned for the bartender. "This is a lovely surprise."

Before I could speak again, the bartender arrived, and Mr. Normand said, "Two white wine spritzers, Barry."

Although I didn't want a white wine spritzer, I let the matter go. Mr. Normand was giving me a wide, shark-like grin, and I wanted to ask my questions and get out.

"I ordered some morels from Janine Harris today," I said, hoping he'd quickly understand that I was here on business. Business...investigating... They were kind of the same thing.

"Morels?"

"Yes. A woman named Brooke recommended Janine. I believe Brooke works here?"

"Used to." Mr. Normand's voice was flat and not as welcoming anymore.

The bartender placed our drinks on coasters in front of us.

"Thank you," I said to the bartender before turning back to Mr. Normand. "Brooke told me you got your foraged mushrooms from Janine and her sons, and I wanted to ask if you were pleased with the quality."

"Yeah, sure, they were fine." He downed half his drink.

"Was it Janine Harris who provided the jack-o-lantern mushrooms instead of the chicken of the woods?" I asked.

He scowled at me. "What are you getting at?"

"I need to know if you trust Ms. Harris and her company to provide safe mushrooms to your customers. If you don't, I'm certainly not serving her mushrooms in my cafe." I took a tiny sip of the white wine spritzer. "Do you still buy from the company despite their misstep?"

Mr. Normand appeared to realize I wasn't there to accuse him of anything, and his scowl became less intense. "No. I haven't bought from them since the mix-up. Plus, I fired my head chef and Brooke."

"Oh, I didn't realize..."

"So, are you and Brooke friends?"

"No," I said. "I met her yesterday when I went to the farmers' market to confront Helen Madison." Although I hadn't met Brooke at the farmers' market, I thought that was an efficient way to bring Helen into the conversation and avoid a long, drawn-out explanation as to how I'd met Brooke.

"That's right. Helen made some sort of stink at your restaurant, didn't she?"

"Made a stink?" I scoffed. "She shut us down on Friday afternoon. Plus, I think she might've followed me out of Brea Ridge last night."

"Sorry to hear that. I know firsthand how devastating an unfortunate incident can be to a business."

"You said that after the snafu with the mushrooms, you fired both the head chef and Brooke. Why those two?"

"Well, the head chef had to go after all those people got sick," he said.

"Even though he might've simply made an honest mistake?"

He drained his glass and signaled for another. "It wasn't his first mistake--more like his last chance. Besides, we needed to let him go to try to salvage our reputation."

"And Brooke?"

"She's the one who accepted delivery of the mushrooms. And she definitely should have known better."

"Where do you purchase your mushrooms now, Mr. Normand?"

"I buy online from a reputable site." He took a pen from his pocket and wrote the website address on a napkin. "Think twice about buying from Janine."

"I will," I said. "Thank you."

"And come back anytime." He winked.

I managed a stiff smile as I left. How was this guy friends with our sweet Walter?

I still had some time to kill before meeting with Janine, so I drove home. When I pulled into the

Gayle Leeson

driveway, I noticed both Roger's truck and Jackie's car at the big house. Was something wrong? I quickly checked my phone to make sure I hadn't missed any messages or calls. I hadn't.

Hurrying inside, I grabbed Rory and his leash, and the two of us walked to the big house. We entered through the kitchen door and found Jackie standing at the stove.

"Hi. What's cooking?"

"I'm making spaghetti and garlic knots for Granny and Roger," she said. "Aunt Jenna went out with Clark. You're welcome to join us for dinner."

"Cool."

She narrowed her eyes. "You're up to something. What is it?"

"I'm not up to anything. I promise."

Rory barked.

Rolling my eyes as if my dog had called my bluff, I said, "Okay, fine. I might be up to a little something."

"Spill it." Jackie blew into the pot to keep the pasta from boiling over and then placed her wooden spoon over the top.

"I went to see Janine Harris after work and told her I'd like to buy some morels."

Aunt Bess sashayed into the kitchen in time to hear me. "Did you say you're trying to buy morals? Hmph. I know good and well you were raised with all kinds of morals. If you've lost them, it's no fault of anybody in this family."

"Mushrooms, Aunt Bess. I'm talking about mushrooms."

"I figured as much." She grinned. "I was just yanking your chain. That's what the cool kids call giving somebody a hard time." She looked down at Rory. "Why, there's my Rory-bear. I haven't seen you in a month of Sundays. Let's see what I can find you to eat."

"He doesn't need anything, Aunt Bess. I'm going to take him back home and feed him in a few minutes."

"Oh, fiddlesticks. He can't come visit his Aunt Bess without getting a little spoiling while he's here." She opened the refrigerator and got Rory a cube of cheese. "He can have this bite of cheese, can't he?"

Without waiting for my response—which would have been yes, by the way—she gave Rory the cheese. He wolfed it down gratefully.

Roger came into the kitchen, and I had to let go of Rory's leash as he ran to dance around Roger's feet.

Scooping him up, Roger said, "Hey, buddy. You keeping Amy out of trouble? You're not? Well, that's a tough job for anybody."

I poked my tongue out at him.

"Would you mind hanging out with Granny for a little while after supper?" Jackie asked him. "I'm going with Amy to buy some mushrooms."

"Sure."

Aunt Bess clapped her hands together. "Any chance you and I could go dancing?"

"Maybe. We'll see how long the other gals will be gone." He sat Rory back onto the floor. "When will supper be ready?"

"About fifteen minutes," Jackie said.

"Good. I've got time to show Amy my plans for the his and her offices," he said.

"Correction." I picked up Rory's leash. "His office and her fancy room."

Chapter Sixteen

Jackie drove us to Janine's farm. Roger was familiar with the area and had said Jackie's SUV was better equipped to handle the gravel road leading to the farm, which was located on the outskirts of Winter Garden. Remembering the one time I'd taken the Bug to Landon Farms, I agreed.

"Thank you for driving," I told Jackie. "I'll pay to get your car washed when we get back to town."

"No problem. Tell me again how you became acquainted with Brooke."

I explained how Mom and I had met Brooke's daughter, Ruthie, at the nursing home while visiting Mildred. "Ruthie hadn't been aware of Wood Bradford's death, and she said her mom used to work with Mr. Bradford. I asked her to see if her mom would discuss Mr. Bradford with us, and she agreed."

"And Brooke told you she left Epic Eats because it wasn't the same after Bradford went out on his own?"

"That's what she said, but today, Mr. Normand told me he fired Brooke because she accepted the jack-o-lantern mushrooms as chicken of the woods mushrooms."

Jackie stopped to allow a squirrel to dart across the road in front of us. "And why are we buying morels from Janine again?"

"My initial thought was to have them tested to see if they are, in fact, black morels and not some false morels."

"Do you really think she'd stay in business if she consistently sold the wrong mushrooms?" Jackie asked.

"No." I sighed. "I don't really know what I'm doing, Jackie. I'm just desperate to find out who knows what and to determine who might've killed Wood Bradford so we can salvage our reputation. "You, Scott, and I have worked too hard to see the cafe fall apart now."

"That's not going to happen. Business was great Saturday and today. People know the cafe, and they trust us."

"To an extent. But I can't help feeling as if Helen Madison cast a shadow over us, and I want the truth to come out."

"So do I." Jackie tapped her fingers on the steering wheel. "Let's see what we can learn about Brooke from Janine."

When we reached the farm, there was a sign by the front gate warning that there were guard dogs on duty and instructing delivery people to leave items there. All other visitors were instructed to honk their horns and to remain in their vehicles to await assistance.

Jackie sounded the horn.

Within seconds, four Great Pyrenees arrived at the gate.

"Good grief," Jackie said. "Plan B. Who cares what Janine knows about Brooke? Let's forget the mushrooms."

"I prefer Plan A."

"When I suggested Plan A, I didn't realize the woman we were hoping to interrogate had a pack of dire wolves."

Janine arrived, opened the gate, and called out over the barking dogs, "Drive on up to the house! I'll join you there!"

Jackie eased the SUV through the open gate and slowly drove on up the driveway. "I'm not getting out."

"That's okay. I will."

After Janine closed the gate and walked up the driveway, I called, "Is it safe to get out?"

"Sure," Janine said. "Move slowly and stand still for a moment to let the dogs sniff you. Try not to act afraid or make any sudden movements."

"Good luck," Jackie muttered under her breath.

I opened the car door and was met by a dog whose head was at the height of my rib cage as soon as I stepped onto the ground. "Hello, gorgeous."

The dog sniffed me, wagged his tail and promptly sat on my feet.

"Gabe, get off her." Janine came to stand beside Gabe. "She can't even move."

"May I pet him?"

She laughed. "If you don't, he'll sit there all night."

After letting Gabe smell my hand, I stroked his shoulder. "You're a good boy."

He wagged his tail harder and then leapt up to put his massive front paws on my shoulders and licked the side of my face.

I laughed. "Wow, you're such a big boy!"

"He doesn't usually do that to strangers," Janine said. "You must be special."

"Thank you, Gabe. I like you too."

"Come on," Janine said to the dog. "Get down now."

One of the other dogs came around the side of the SUV. He sniffed me, uttered a low growl, and then stalked a short distance away.

"Everything is okay, Michael." Janine went over to him and patted his head. "Amy is going to be visiting us for a little while."

At her soothing tone, Michael lay down but continued to watch me.

"He won't hurt you," Janine told me, "unless, of course, you threaten a member of his family. They're all sweet dogs to us, but they take their guardianship role very seriously. Especially Michael." She jerked her head toward the SUV. "Doesn't your friend want to get out?"

I turned and looked at Jackie, who remained behind the wheel with her seat belt still buckled. I motioned for her to get out. She shook her head.

The other two dogs ventured over to check me out. One was standoffish, although not to the extent Michael was. The other was friendly, but again, not to the degree Gabe was.

"What are their names?" I asked, as I petted the friendly one.

"The one you're petting is Deborah. The other female is Janel." She laughed at the bemused expression I'd obviously made. "You're wondering why my dogs have such weird names. Since they're guardians, I wanted them to have strong, majestic names. Gabriel and Michael, after the archangels, and Deborah and Jael, after women warriors in the Bible."

"That's really cool," I said.

"Come on, and I'll get you those morels."

I took one last look over my shoulder at Jackie, but it was clear she wasn't coming. I was confused. Fearless Jackie, who never backed down from a challenge and had never—to my knowledge—been afraid of dogs, sat gripping the steering wheel. Surely, she wouldn't leave me. Would she?

Following Janine into the farmhouse, I said, "I spoke with Jim Normand today. He told me he fired Brooke for accepting those mushrooms."

"I don't blame him. I'd have done the same thing." She handed me a paper bag. "Go ahead and check those."

I took a handful of morels from the bag. "These look great."

"Thank you. Jim Normand wouldn't be in the legal trouble he's in if he hadn't hired some inexperienced kid in order to save a dollar."

It dawned on me that Janine Harris wasn't a co-defendant in the food poisoning lawsuit. I made a mental note to ask Sarah if the "inexperienced kid" was named.

"Was Mr. Normand right then that Brooke should have been able to identify the mushrooms?"

"Of course, she should have. She and I used to help our mothers forage together when we were still in elementary school." She absently stroked the ear of the dog standing beside her. "But I wasn't there, and I have no idea what happened. She might not have even looked at the mushrooms."

"At the post office, you asked me to keep my visit to you quiet," I said. "Why is that?"

"I'm trying to get out of the foraging business. Even though I had nothing to do with that food poisoning incident at Epic Eats, it soured me on the whole business. From now on, I'll forage for personal use, but that's it."

Holding the bag aloft, I said, "Thank you for selling me these."

"You're welcome. I had a surplus."

I turned to go but had a thought and faced her again. "Homer Pickens mentioned that you saw a man arguing with Wood Bradford at the food truck shortly before Mr. Bradford collapsed. Was that man Jim Normand?"

"It was," she said. "But you didn't hear that from me."

"Do you think Mr. Normand is dangerous?"

She didn't directly answer my question. "I prefer not to get involved in other people's business, Amy. I suggest you do likewise."

"I wish I could; but after Helen Madison came into my cafe, stood on a chair, and announced to a dining room full of patrons that I and the rest of my staff poisoned Wood Bradford, I'm determined to find out who killed the man and to salvage the reputation of the Down South Cafe."

"I'm sorry that happened to you," she said. "I don't know Helen personally, but I've heard she has more issues than Southern Living. Nobody with good sense will take her seriously."

"If only I could be sure of that."

"Trust me. It'll blow over. Do yourself a favor and let the police investigate Wood's murder."

Chapter Seventeen

Jackie drove carefully down the driveway, and we both waved goodbye to Janine as we passed through the gate.

"How'd it go?" Jackie asked.

"Fine. Janine said Brooke should have recognized the mushrooms. They foraged together when they were children."

"Maybe Brooke didn't keep it up and forgot everything she ever knew. Unlikely, but possible."

"Would you mind if I call Sarah?" I asked. "I have a quick question for her."

"No. Go ahead."

I called Sarah and told her, "You're on speaker with Jackie and me."

"Hey, Jackie," Sarah said. "What's new?"

"Not much," Jackie answered. "Just chauffeuring Amy around to meet dire wolves and buy possibly toxic mushrooms."

"Dire wolves?" Sarah asked.

"Great Pyrenees," I said. "Four of them. Two were really sweet."

"Even the sweet ones would have turned on you if you'd slapped a mosquito off Janine's face," Jackie said. "I learned a long time ago not to mess with big dogs."

"I agree that they need to be respected, but..." I trailed off, realizing we were wasting Sarah's time. "But I didn't call to talk with you about dogs, Sarah. I wanted to ask you if the person who sold the jack-o-lantern mushrooms to Epic Eats was named in the lawsuit."

"No. The restaurant owners had the burden of ensuring the safety of the food they provided their patrons."

Turning onto the hardtop road, Jackie asked, "Why are we so concerned about the lawsuit and toxic mushrooms if Wood Bradford was poisoned with antifreeze?"

"I'd say there are only three logical answers to that question," Sarah said. "Either the person who killed Wood Bradford doesn't know how to identify toxic mushrooms, that's what they want the authorities to believe, or the toxic mushrooms have nothing to do with Wood's murder and chasing down that lead is a waste of time."

After talking with Sarah, Jackie and I decided to call Scott. He told us to bring the mushrooms to his place and that he'd call Ivy to see if she could join us.

"You don't have to take me to Scott's apartment," I told Jackie. "I know you're eager to get back to Roger and Aunt Bess."

"You're not getting rid of me that easily," she said. "Granny and Roger are doing fine. I don't doubt that they're getting into mischief, but I know they're all right."

"You know I don't want to get rid of you. I just didn't want to leave Roger in the lurch."

"Roger adores Granny. They have a blast together."

"True. But it's still not like spending time with you."

She laughed. "Thank goodness for that, I guess. But I'm guessing Granny was a lot like me when she was young."

"I can see that."

"I appreciate Aunt Jenna more than you know." She turned her face away, presumably to look at something on the left side of the road. "She takes awfully good care of Granny."

"Aunt Bess took good care of Nana before she passed," I said. "Mom and I appreciate her doing that." I paused a moment. "That's what family does. We take care of each other the best that we can."

"Okay. Don't go getting sappy on me."

I huffed. "You started it."

"There are no witnesses, and I'll never admit to it. I'm not sentimental in the least."

"Scott will believe me," I teased.

"Of course, he will. He always does."

"That's because I'm always right." It felt good to be joking with Jackie again. I felt like we were back on track, or at least getting there.

Scott's apartment was eclectic. While the living room was filled with mismatched furniture, an enormous television, and two different gaming systems, the kitchen was minimal and pristine. I knew from having been there before that Scott's cabinets were stocked with a wide variety of baking pans and that he had a drawer dedicated to carefully arranged cake decorating tips. The man enjoyed relaxing in the living room, but he was all business when it came to his kitchen.

He and Ivy were sitting on the sofa when Jackie and I arrived. We all greeted each other, and Scott offered us something to drink.

"Nothing for me," I said, sinking onto an armchair adjacent to the sofa.

"I'd love a glass of water." Jackie followed Scott into the kitchen.

Ivy nodded at the paper bag I was holding. "Are those the morels?"

"Yes." I handed her the bag.

She took the bag, opened it, and retrieved a couple of the morels. "These are black morels, all right. Nice ones too."

"You don't need to run any tests or anything?"

"No." She smiled. "I've done my fair share of foraging for mushrooms in my day."

"Yeah." Scott ambled back into the living room. "Ivy knows all about the shrooms." He returned to his seat on the sofa. "I found some while I was living in Arizona. I sent her a pic, and she told me to throw them away immediately."

"They were scaly caps, you big lug." She punched her brother playfully on the shoulder. "Those wouldn't have killed you, but they sure would've made you sick."

"Thanks for having my back, as usual," he said.

I smiled at Jackie, who was standing in the doorway between the living room and the kitchen drinking a glass of water. We always had each other's backs too, when push came to shove.

Ivy dropped the morels back into the bag and held it out toward me.

Holding up a hand, I said, "If you'd like to have those, you're welcome to them."

"You don't want them?" she asked.

I shook my head. "I've always relied on store-bought mushrooms."

"You don't know what you're missing. Black morels are delicious." She paused. "They're expensive too. Let me buy them from you."

"Nothing doing. I'm just glad you're taking them and that they aren't going to waste."

Jackie finished her water, took her glass back into the kitchen, and then returned to lean against the door jamb. "Amy, Sarah, and I were discussing this situation over the phone on the drive here, but I'd like your take on it, Ivy. How is it that Wood Bradford was killed with antifreeze when there are all these people with expert knowledge of toxic mushrooms hanging around him?"

"Well, it's simple, isn't it?" Ivy placed the bag of mushrooms on the coffee table beside one of Scott's game controllers. "Either the person who poisoned Wood Bradford knows nothing about mushrooms, wanted to disguise their knowledge of mushrooms, or couldn't find anything toxic enough to do the job within a particular time frame."

"Oh, we hadn't considered that last one," I said. "Based on your knowledge of antifreeze poisoning, how long do you think it took for Mr. Bradford to succumb to the poison?"

"We haven't received the autopsy report yet to know if Mr. Bradford had any preexisting conditions or health factors that contributed to his death, but I'd estimate ingestion to have been around two days before he died."

"Two days?" Jackie asked. "Then we're completely in the clear."

"From a legal standpoint, we are," I said. "But the public doesn't know that because it's still unconfirmed that Wood Bradford didn't die from ingesting our pastries. We can't clear our name until the killer is caught."

"We're working on that," Ivy said. "You three need to go back to concentrating on the cafe and making your delicious food. Leave the investigating to us—the professionals."

I exchanged glances with Jackie and Scott. Sure, we'd concentrate on the cafe, but there was no way we would stop investigating.

Chapter Eighteen

Jackie and I returned to the big house.

"Where have y'all been?" Aunt Bess demanded, as we walked into the living room. "I know It didn't take you this long to go pick up a bag of mushrooms."

"We took the morels over to Scott's place and gave them to Ivy." I took a seat on the rocking chair next to Aunt Bess.

She nearly gave herself whiplash turning to look at me. "You took the mushrooms to Ivy? Are they evidence? I thought Wood Bradford died from antifreeze poisoning. Is that just what the police are telling people so there's not widespread panic over mushrooms?"

"Granny, if you'd take a breath, we could answer your questions." Jackie sank onto the sofa beside Roger and gave him a mischievous grin. "What have you two been into while we were gone?"

Before Roger could attempt to answer Jackie's question, Aunt Bess said, "Jacqueline Fonseca, you and Amy had better answer my questions right this minute!"

"After having Ivy confirm that the mushrooms were, in fact, black morels, I let her have them," I said. "They weren't evidence. I've never cooked with anything except store-bought mushrooms, and Ivy really likes the taste of morels, so I gave them to her."

"Morels are delicious as long as you get them from somebody who knows their mushrooms," Roger said. "I love them sautéed in butter."

"I'm sorry. I didn't realize you liked them, Roger. I'd have divided them between you and Ivy."

"That's all right, Flowerpot. I—"

"Tell me what's going on with the mushrooms and the investigation," Aunt Bess interrupted. "No more beating around the bush."

Between us, Jackie and I managed to bring Aunt Bess and Roger up to speed on our trip to Janine's farm.

"I'm glad she's got those big dogs out there for protection," Aunt Bess said. "Especially now that her husband is gone."

"Janine didn't poison him with bad mushrooms, did she, Granny?" Jackie winked.

"No." She paused. "She might ought to have though." At our shocked expressions, she added, "Only a little bit. Enough to give him a stomachache and the runs, not to kill him. He ran off to West Virginia and left her to raise those boys alone."

"We didn't see Janine's sons while we were there," I said. "But I don't think they did the mushroom foraging for Jim Normand. I believe the forager who procured the mushrooms for Epic Eats must have been a freelancer."

"Yeah, she told Amy that the whole food poisoning episode soured her on selling to the public period," Jackie said.

"She also said that Brooke, a woman who worked at Epic Eats, should have known the difference between jack-o-lantern and chicken of the woods mushrooms." I gently rocked the chair. "And, in fact, Jim Normand fired both Brooke and the chef after the food poisoning incident because he felt they should have caught the error—an error that is currently getting Epic Eats sued."

"Why are we investigating the food poisoning?" Aunt Bess steepled her fingers together, the wheels obviously spinning under her cottony head of hair. "And does this Brooke have a daughter who works at Mildred's nursing home?"

"We aren't investigating the food poisoning exactly," I said. "We're just trying to talk with people who might've known Wood Bradford and his associates so they can point us in the direction of the murderer. Oh, and yes, Brooke does have a daughter who works at the nursing home. Her name is Ruthie, and in fact, she's how we met Brooke. Why?"

"That's Brooke Shipley." She threw a look of disgust in Jackie's direction. "She was in your mother's graduating class. Made trouble for Renee all through school."

"What kind of trouble?" I asked.

"Telling tales on her, making fun of her, that sort of thing. Brooke was always sticking her nose where it didn't belong." She shook her head. "I can't help but wonder If she's not part of the reason your mother got on drugs."

"I don't know about that," Jackie said. "I'd imagine Mom gave back as good as she got. She never was a doormat."

"Yeah, well, I still reckon that Brooke is one to keep an eye on anyway," Aunt Bess said.

I rested my head against the back of the rocking chair. "It sure seems like Woodrow Bradford and Jim Normand surrounded themselves with some pretty nutty women. Brooke, Helen Madison..."

"Helen Madison?" Roger echoed.

"Yeah." Jackie turned to look at him. "She's the one who threw the fit at the cafe. I told you about her."

"You ranted to me about a psycho named Helen who had a tantrum in the cafe, but you didn't tell me it was Helen Madison."

"And? You know her?" Jackie asked.

"A little," Roger said. "My crew and I built a porch onto her mom's house a couple of years ago. She needed the old one replaced with one that was handicap accessible."

"Why would Helen need a handicap ramp?" Aunt Bess asked. "According to Jackie, she scurried up onto that chair like a squirrel."

"She didn't need the ramp," Roger answered. "Her mother did."

"Helen lives with her mother?" Jackie asked. "At her age?"

Given her feelings about Helen, nothing the woman did was going to go unscrutinized.

"If Helen's mother is elderly, it makes sense that Helen might live with her." I was trying to help Roger out. "I believe what we're all wondering, Roger, is what impression did you get of Helen while you were working at her mom's place?"

"That's exactly what we want to know." Aunt Bess gave him a firm nod. "Did you come across any bones buried beneath that porch?"

"Sorry, but I didn't find any bones, Aunt Bess, and her mom lives by herself, as far as I know. Helen was just there to supervise the work."

"Well, it is more likely any victims would be buried in the backyard rather than the front." Aunt Bess frowned. "I don't suppose you had any reason to dig around in the backyard?"

"I'm afraid not, but you're right. Most people bury bodies in their backyard as opposed to the front where just anybody might drive by and see them." To his credit, Roger kept a straight face while making this observation.

Jackie scoffed. "Did Helen Madison strike you as a psycho, or not?"

"I dunno. She didn't strike me as the type of person who'd fly into a rage and destroy someone's sourdough loaves or any—"

Roger broke off, as Jackie clobbered him over the head with a throw pillow. He laughed and tried to shield his head with his arms.

"Jackie was provoked!" Aunt Bess shouted above the commotion.

"Then or now?" I called back.

"Both!"

The altercation between Jackie and Roger, such as it was, ended when Mom and Clark arrived.

"It appears we've interrupted a public flogging," Clark said, as he helped Mom out of her jacket.

Jackie had the grace to look the tiniest bit sheepish as she fluffed her weapon of choice and returned it to the corner of the sofa. "Did you guys have fun?"

"We did," Mom said. "Clark, would you like something to drink?"

"No, love, I need to go. I've got several early appointments tomorrow." Clark smiled at all of us. "I just wanted to walk Jenna inside and wish all you folks a goodnight."

"Take it easy, Clark," Roger said. "Thanks for the rescue." He shot a look at Aunt Bess. "That's more than I can say for you, Little Miss Take-Me-For-Ice Cream."

"What can I say, darlin'?" Aunt Bess shrugged. "Blood is thicker than ice cream...but only a teensy bit."

After Clark left, I followed Mom into the kitchen and filled her in on the afternoon's events.

She made each of us a cup of decaf coffee and set out a sleeve of shortbread cookies.

Spooning creamer into her cup, she said, "You need to speak with the chef Jim Normand fired."

"True." I dipped a cookie into my coffee. "The trouble is I don't know who he is or where to find him."

Her lips curved into a slight smile. "If I find out, may I go with you to interview him?"

Laughing, I said, "You really have caught the sleuthing bug! And, yes, if you find him, we'll go talk with him together."

Chapter Nineteen

I was preparing the lunch special when Mom called. She began the call with, "I found him."

Focused on chopping the onion in front of me, I drew a blank. "Found who?"

"The chef who was fired from Epic Eats after the food poisoning Incident."

I stopped chopping. "Seriously? That was quick."

"Tell me about it. You said it yourself last night, I'm getting the hang of this detective work."

Although I was pretty sure that's not what I'd said, I didn't say so.

"You know, I'm not that old," she continued. "I could probably go to the police academy and--"

"Mom, what's the man's name, and where do we find him?"

"Sorry. Didn't mean to prattle on."

I felt a slight stab of guilt but brushed it away. It was the middle of a workday, and the lunch rush was about to start.

"His name is Pete Lloyd, and he's working at a barbecue place in Brea Ridge," she said. "I'll pick you up, and we'll go there after you close up."

"Great," I said. "I'm looking forward to it."

"So am I." I could hear the excitement in her voice. "I'm writing some questions on index cards."

"Getting prepared—good thinking," I said. "See you soon."

Jackie was looking at me as I pressed the button on the side of my headset and ended the call. "What is it you're looking forward to?"

"Mom located the chef who used to work at Epic Eats. She and I are going to Brea Ridge to talk with him after work."

"Well, I haven't met Mr. Normand yet, so I believe I'll go chat with him." She grinned. "Maybe he can tell me where I can find some good mushrooms."

"Fair warning—Jim Normand seems to think he's a ladies' man."

"Good to know." She resumed rolling out pizza dough. "I'm all for creative recipes, but how well received do you think our special of the day is going to be?"

"If our patrons don't embrace our apple butter pizza, then at least we all know what we're having for dinner this evening."

Mom arrived as I was wiping down the counter.

"I'll be ready in a minute, Mom."

Jackie breezed out of the kitchen wearing a denim jacket and a leather tote slung over one shoulder. "You know, I kinda wish our pizza had been less of a hit. Now I'm going to have to make one for Roger and me when I get home. Oh, well, I'm off. Wish me luck! I'll let you know how it goes."

She left without stopping for our wishes.

"Why does she need luck for making the pizza?" Mom asked.

"That's not what she needs luck with. She's going to see Jim Normand and do a little investigating of her own."

Mom frowned. "Do you think that's wise? Sending Jackie on a fact-finding mission alone?"

"It was her idea, and I wasn't about to suggest that it might not be a good one," I said. "I also didn't try to give her any pointers."

"And if she winds up squashing Jim Normand's sourdough?"

I chuckled. "Given the little I know about Mr. Normand, I'd assume he had it coming."

The barbecue restaurant where Pete Lloyd now worked looked as if it had seen better days. I thought about the understated elegance of Epic Eats and felt bad for the chef. After all, he hadn't foraged the mushrooms; he'd merely trusted that they were the right ones.

Mom and I had decided on the drive to Brea Ridge that we'd get a takeout order after speaking with Mr. Lloyd. That should keep him out of hot water with his new employer while also emphasizing the fact that we didn't believe his cooking was at fault for the food poisoning incident.

We left the Bug in the sparsely filled lot and walked inside the restaurant. The dull brown and orange interior was as uninspired as the exterior. I knew, though, that looks could be deceiving; or, at least, I hoped they were, especially if we were planning on buying food at this establishment. A quick glance at Mom told me she was expecting the worst.

"Sit wherever you'd like," a bored-sounding waitress called from somewhere within the restaurant. "I'll be with you in a minute."

Mom headed for the booth closest to us—and to the door—and I followed her.

Sitting across from her, I inhaled the smoky, sweet aroma of the barbecue. "It smells good."

"Mmm-hmm." She looked as if she were ready to bolt at any second.

The waitress approached in sneakers that squeaked against the floor with every other step. "What can I get you?"

"We're actually here to speak with Pete Lloyd, if he's in today," I said.

He was. Mom had called to confirm it before coming to the cafe to pick me up.

With a shrug, the waitress turned and shouted, "Pete, there's somebody here to see you!" Then she trudged away; whether it was to attend to other customers or to go out back for a smoke break, we never knew because we didn't see her again.

A middle-aged man emerged from the kitchen wearing a long white apron and a skull cap. He was wiping his hand on a paper towel and surveying the dining room, presumably to see who wanted to speak with him.

Giving him a wave, I asked, "Mr. Lloyd?"

"Yeah." He lumbered over to our table. "Call me Pete. What can I do for you?"

I scooted over so he could take a seat on the bench beside me. "Could you sit with us for a moment? I promise we'll be brief."

"Sure." He sat beside me and looked at both Mom and me appraisingly.

"My name is Amy Flowers, and this is my mother, Jenna."

Pete said it was nice to meet us, and we returned the sentiment before I continued.

"I'm sorry for what happened to you at Epic Eats."

"Sssh!" His eyes darted around the restaurant. "Could we keep that on the down-low please? Nobody here knows about that."

"Sorry," I said. "I just wanted to see what you thought about Woodrow Bradford and some of your former co-workers."

"Wood was a decent enough guy . . . In the beginning."

"In the beginning?" Mom echoed. "What changed?"

"Well, I started noticing little things at first. Like the way he'd flirt with Helen and then push her away when she took him seriously. It struck me as mean. If he wasn't interested in her, he shouldn't lead her on."

"Helen Madison, you mean?" I asked.

He nodded. "But the main thing that turned me against Wood was the way he let Brooke and me take the blame for that entire mushroom fiasco. I'm not saying that either one of us was blameless--Brooke should've recognized that they were the wrong mushrooms, and I should have double checked with somebody before baking them up into that casserole--but the man who supplied the mushrooms should've shouldered his share of the responsibility instead of hanging us out to dry."

I blinked. "Are you saying Wood Bradford provided the jack-o-lantern mushrooms to Epic Eats?" Surely, Pete had to have been mistaken. "Mr. Bradford wasn't even working at Epic Eats then, was he?"

"No, he wasn't, but Brooke told me he's the one who brought us the mushrooms."

As I sat there slack-jawed, Mom took over the interview. "Is that something Mr. Bradford did often—supply mushrooms to Epic Eats?"

"As far as I know, that's the only time he ever did," Pete said.

"And, yet, he wasn't named in the lawsuit," I mused.

Pete's voice had an edge to it now. "He threw the rest of us under the bus and never looked back."

We thanked Pete for his time and gave him our takeout order. When he went to the kitchen to prepare our food, I rubbed my forehead.

"Mr. Bradford might not have been as nice as we'd thought," I told Mom.

"I'm wondering what his motivation was in providing those toxic mushrooms," she said. "Do you think he gave them to Epic Eats on purpose?"

"Maybe." I took out my phone.

"What are you doing?"

"I'm texting Jackie to tell her the latest and to have her ask Jim Normand about it."

Raising her brows, she said, "You know Jackie won't handle the situation delicately."

"I know. If we need to smash a gnat with a sledgehammer, so be it. We need to cut through the lies and the coverups and find out who killed Woodrow Bradford and why."

Chapter Twenty

Ryan, Mom, Aunt Bess, Jackie, and I gathered at the big house for our barbecue dinner. Both Clark and Roger had to work. Too bad for them, since the meal was better than I'd expected it to be. In fact, it was delicious. We had some burnt ends, chopped brisket, sliced turkey, fried green tomatoes, and potato salad.

Over dinner, we compared notes, starting with what Jackie had learned from Jim Normand.

"Normand claims he doesn't know who provided the mushrooms," she said. "If Wood Bradford brought the mushrooms, it's news to him."

"Did you believe him?" Aunt Bess slid another fried green tomato onto her plate. "If he's a cold-blooded killer, he's probably a decent liar to boot."

"I did believe him." She sipped her iced tea. "He also said he hated firing Pete because Pete was the best chef he ever had."

"Judging by this meal, Pete certainly is good at his job," Ryan said. "I still don't understand why Normand felt it was imperative to fire Pete if Pete wasn't the one who procured the mushrooms, though."

"He told me he felt it would look bad if he put the blame fully on Brooke," Jackie said. "But it's clear that's where he thinks the blame lies. He said she always bragged about how well she knew mushrooms, and then when it truly counted, she failed to keep a family from eating toxic jack-o-lantern mushrooms."

I deliberated on the fairness of what happened to Pete as I took a second helping of potato salad. "I do understand Mr. Normand's thought process here. As a chef and an owner, I feel responsible for the food eaten at the cafe. If we were to hire an outside chef who prepared something that made people sick, I'd feel compelled to fire that person. But, on the other hand, the onus to make sure the food provided is of an excellent quality is on the owner. It seems Brooke might have been the one treated unfairly."

"Maybe so, but Normand trusted her, and her mistake is costing him big time." Jackie gestured with her fork. "If the family settles out of court, this lawsuit will end up costing Normand hundreds of thousands of dollars. If they don't settle, he'll have to file bankruptcy and will lose everything."

"Did the partnership between Mr. Normand and Mr. Bradford end amicably?" Mom asked.

"Normand said it did, but I'm not sure I'm buying that," Jackie said.

Ryan frowned. "Why not?"

Shaking her head, Jackie said, "I'm not sure. It was just a gut feeling."

"That's a feeling you learn to trust in my business," Ryan said.

Aunt Bess nodded. "We do indeed, sweetie."

"Also, Janine said she saw Mr. Normand arguing with Mr. Bradford on the day of the murder," I said. "But she didn't want anyone to know she said so."

Then I filled everyone in on what Pete had told us.

"The Sheriff's office needs to take formal statements from both Pete and Brooke," Ryan said. "We hadn't yet connected either of them to Wood Bradford's murder, but if the firing was because—as Pete alleged—Bradford threw them under the bus, then they both have motive. Thanks for your help, ladies."

"You're most welcome," Aunt Bess said.

"What about Mr. Normand?" I asked. "Isn't he a suspect?"

"He's always been a suspect but not a very strong one." He rubbed his chin. "I think we should talk with him again after speaking with Brooke and Pete."

"I can be there, if you need me," Aunt Bess said. "Jackie and Amy both mentioned that Mr. Normand fancies himself a ladies' man."

"Thank you, Aunt Bess. I appreciate the offer, but I don't like the idea of any of you putting yourselves in danger. Amy, Jenna, and Jackie uncovered some valuable information, but I feel the police should handle the investigation from here on out."

"Well, if you say so." Aunt Bess took another slice of turkey. "For the record, I believe Pete is innocent because this barbecue is too good to have been made by a killer. Mean people generally don't make decent barbecue."

As Ryan and I curled up on the sofa with the pets on our laps, talk turned to our upcoming wedding.

"Mom sent me some photos of mother-of-the-groom dresses she likes," Ryan said. "She wanted me to give her my opinion and get yours. I think they all look nice, but I can't see much difference."

"I honestly don't care what anyone wears." I kissed the top of Rory's head.

With a sigh, Ryan said, "If I tell Mom you don't care about her dress, she's gonna be pretty upset."

"Oh, no, sweetheart, I didn't mean it like that! I only meant that as long as our friends and family are there, they can wear their pajamas for all I care. All that really matters is that I'm marrying you."

He nodded. "I'll tell her you want her to wear pjs."

I playfully slapped his arm and got a warning me-ow from Princess Eloise. "She'll look gorgeous in anything. Forward the photos to me, and I'll text or call her tomorrow."

"Thanks." He gave me a quick peck on the lips. "I'm kinda liking the pj thing, though. Wonder if anyone makes a flannel tuxedo?"

"I imagine Amanda Tucker of Designs on You could fix you up."

Rory stiffened and his ears perked up as he watched the door. He uttered a low growl before hopping off my lap and running toward the door, barking for all he was worth.

Princess Eloise fled the room.

"Something's out there." I stood.

Ryan got to his feet and stepped in front of me. "Careful. It's probably nothing, but let me check it out."

He went to the door, looked out the window, and then opened the door and stepped onto the porch, careful not to let Rory slip out in the process. "Ms. Madison? May I help you?"

I scooped Rory into my arms and stood at the screen door, eager to hear what Helen Madison had to say.

"I came to apologize," she said, bunching the hem of her shirt in both hands.

"You can come on inside," I said. "If you're uncomfortable around dogs, I can put Rory in the bedroom."

"Oh, I love dogs." She stepped closer to the porch. "As long as they don't bite."

"He won't." I moved back into the living room, allowing Ryan and Helen to come inside.

Once we'd invited Helen into the house, Rory became an armful of wiggles. I placed him back on the floor, and he went to greet our guest.

Helen stooped down to pet him. "What a sweet boy you are! Yes, you are!"

Rory licked the tip of her nose, and she laughed.

Ryan and I sat on the couch, and I gestured for Helen to have a seat on the armchair. She sat down, looked at us, and immediately began wringing her hands.

"Ms. Madison, you have no reason to be nervous," Ryan said, "although we would like to know how you found Amy's house and why you were hanging around outside."

"I followed her home from Brea Ridge the other night."

"But I didn't come home," I said. "I drove to the police station because I was being followed." My voice sounded sharper than I'd intended.

"I know, but I...I parked on the street near the municipal building and followed you the rest of the way when you left." She ran a trembling hand over her face. "I was standing outside because I was trying to get the nerve to knock."

Rory apparently decided this woman was too uptight for his taste, and he hopped back onto the sofa between Ryan and me.

"Now that you're here, how can we help you?" Ryan asked Helen.

He had adopted his "good cop" voice, and I was glad of that. Although her demeanor made me feel sorry for her, I still didn't trust Helen and wasn't feeling particularly solicitous toward her.

"Please don't press charges against me for trespassing in your cafe." Helen's tear-filled eyes bore into mine. "I'm awfully sorry I acted so rash, and I'll pay back the income you lost that day. Just please don't have me arrested."

"I'm not going to have you arrested, Helen," I said. "And I'm not going to ask you to pay any restitution either. As far as I'm concerned, the matter is behind us."

"Are you sure? Mr. Normand is really upset with me. He wants me to make things right with you before I cause him any more trouble."

I looked at Ryan and then back to Helen. "I don't understand. Why would your actions cause Mr. Normand trouble?"

"I don't know, but he has enough to deal with because of the lawsuit hanging over his head without my making matters worse." She sniffled. "You and your friends are snooping around because of the scene I made at your café; and if I cause him any further aggravation, I'll regret it."

"Okay, I'll admit I probably shouldn't have been snooping—as you put it—around Epic Eats, but I'm trying to find out who killed Wood Bradford." I mainly said the part about shouldn't have been snooping for Ryan's benefit, although he knows me well enough to understand why I'd snooped and to realize I might feel compelled to do it again. "I believe Mr. Bradford's killer needs to be brought to justice and that the blight on the Down South Cafe needs to be removed."

"The Sheriff's Office is thoroughly investigating Mr. Bradford's murder and will have a suspect in custody soon." Ryan's voice sounded less "good cop" than before.

Turning toward him, I placed a hand on his arm. "You and your team are doing a fantastic job. I just enjoy being useful."

"I appreciate that your heart is in the right place, but as Ms. Madison is telling you, you can't always foresee the consequences of your actions."

"Please, please don't argue on my account," Helen said. "I'm grateful to everyone for trying to find

Wood's killer, but I promise to stay away from the cafe and your employees, and I beg you to do me the same courtesy. Stay away from Epic Eats."

Chapter Twenty-One

I was so distracted on Wednesday morning that I burned the first batch of biscuits.

"Get it together, Amy," I scolded myself as I dumped the biscuits into the trash can and started making another batch.

"What's going on with you today?" Scott asked. "You've been jumpy ever since you got here."

"And you're pale." Jackie made this observation as she walked into the kitchen with a basket of strawberries. "Are you sick?"

"No. I didn't sleep well." I paused. "Helen Madison came to my house last night."

"What?"

Jackie and Scott said the word in unison, almost as if they'd rehearsed it.

As I rolled out the biscuit dough, I told them about Helen's visit.

"I can't get over her following you home," Jackie said. "That's plain creepy."

"Thank goodness Ryan was there." Scott spooned brownie batter into a large pan. "Who knows what she might've done had you been alone?"

"She wasn't angry or threatening." I cut out the biscuits and placed them on a baking sheet. "She actually seemed terrified. She begged me not to press trespassing charges against her, and she asked us not to bother Jim Normand anymore. Apparently, he blames her for our snooping around."

Jackie washed the strawberries and then brought them and a small knife to the opposite side of the island from me. "I'm trying to recall everything I said and did yesterday, but Mr. Normand didn't appear to be upset with me."

"He probably wasn't," I said. "I mean, we've all unofficially decided that not only is Helen off her rocker, she's not even sure where the chair is."

Scott put the brownies in one oven and the biscuits in the other, carefully setting the timer on each. "I know you're concerned about the cafe's reputation, Amy-girl--we all are—but too many people who were involved with Wood Bradford are shady characters. I believe you need to take a step back and let our police force do its job."

"I hear what you're saying, Scott, and I know that Ryan, Ivy, Sheriff Billings, and the rest of their force are great at what they do."

"There's a 'but' coming," Jackie muttered.

Frowning at her, I continued, "But Helen is too scared to tell the police whatever it is she knows, or thinks she knows, about Jim Normand. I want to try to get her to tell me what she wouldn't say last night. Then I can tell Ryan, and the police can take it from there." I untied my apron. "Please hold down the fort. I should be back before the lunch rush."

"Where are you going?" Jackie asked.

"To talk with Helen."

"How do you know where to find her?" Scott placed a hand on my shoulder. "The farmers' market isn't open today; and even if it was, it wouldn't be open this early."

"She came to my house, so I'm going to hers," I said. "I saw her address in Ryan's notebook when he wrote up the details of her visit."

"If you go, I'm going with you." Jackie put down the knife. "You said it yourself, Helen is unhinged."

"You need to stay and help Scott. Keep your phone handy. If I need you, I'll call."

Scott took the cinnamon off the shelf. "Text us when you get there."

"And when you leave," Jackie said.

"I will. Thanks, guys."

"Guru Guy is going to wonder where you are." Scott was talking about Homer.

"I'm planning to be back well before he gets here. Wish me luck."

Helen lived in a small house on the outskirts of Brea Ridge. The yard needed mowing, and ninebark shrubs blocked most of the front windows.

I texted Jackie that I'd arrived and was going to knock on the door. Then I got out of the car and did exactly that.

Helen, looking as if she'd rolled out of bed only moments ago, opened the door but left the security chain in place. "What are you doing here? You're gonna get me in trouble."

"I don't want to cause any problems for you, Helen. I believe we want the same thing—to see Wood's killer brought to justice."

"It's not that simple." Her eyes darted from side to side, and I had to fight the impulse to look behind me to make sure there was no one there.

"Please either let me come inside or else come out onto the porch and talk with me," I said.

"No. It's too risky."

"Then just tell me what you know."

She widened her eyes. "No!"

"If you won't tell me, then talk with the police. You obviously believe Jim Normand killed Wood. Maybe if you provide a basis for your belief, the police can arrest him and make him pay for what he did." I stared into her eyes. "Isn't that what you want?"

"Not if it's gonna get me killed, I don't." She pulled her robe tighter around her slender frame. "There's nothing I can do to save Wood. He's gone. I have to look after myself now."

"The police can protect you." I expelled a long breath. "Please, Helen, tell me something the police can use."

"Fine. I'll tell you one thing. The jack-o-lantern mushrooms weren't a mistake. They were an experiment."

"An experiment? What do you mean?"

Helen's response was to shut the door in my face. Knowing she was through talking with me, I went back to the car, texted Jackie that I was on my way back, and drove away.

I arrived back at the Down South Cafe in the midst of the breakfast rush, so I didn't have a chance to talk with Scott and Jackie until after ten o'clock. The cafe was empty of customers and Scott, Jackie, and I were in the kitchen doing the prep work for lunch. Luis was busy bussing tables and putting dishes in the dishwasher.

"So, what happened?" Jackie asked, as she formed hamburger patties and stacked them between squares of wax paper. "The suspense has been about to kill me."

"Me too." Scott was putting together the tuna casserole that was our special of the day.

I told them what had taken place at Helen's house. "The last thing she told me was that the jack-o-lantern mushrooms hadn't been a mistake but an experiment."

"What the heck does that mean?" Jackie asked.

"That was my question to Helen, but she wouldn't answer." I began shredding a head of lettuce.

"If Helen thinks Jim Normand killed Wood Bradford, that cryptic comment about the mushrooms makes no sense," Scott said. "Why would Normand experiment on his customers with toxic mushrooms only to find himself saddled with a lawsuit for food poisoning?"

"I agree," Jackie said. "Besides, didn't Wood provide those mushrooms himself?"

"That's what Pete told Mom and me." I shrugged. "I'm going to pass Helen's information along to Ryan, but I feel that it's probably some nonsense conspiracy theory."

The bell over the door dinged, and I heard Luis greet Homer.

"I'll go." I slipped off my gloves and went into the dining room to see Homer sitting in his usual seat. "Good morning, Homer. Who's your hero today?"

"Hi, Amy. It's the playwright Arthur Miller. He was once married to Marilyn Monroe."

"I'd heard that." I poured Homer a cup of dark roast and placed it on the counter in front of him.

"There was all sorts of speculation about why their marriage broke up," Homer said. "Only they know the truth."

"I imagine you're right about that." I smiled. "I'll get your sausage biscuit."

"Mr. Miller once said that betrayal is the only truth that sticks." Homer's voice trailed after me as I returned to the kitchen.

Wood Bradford had certainly betrayed his fair share of people: Mr. Normand, Helen, Brooke, Pete.... I wondered if one of them hated him enough to kill him over his truth that stuck.

Chapter Twenty-Two

On my drive home from work, I used the hands-free feature in my car to call Ryan.

"Hey, beautiful. What's up?"

"Are you busy?" I asked. "If this is a bad time, we can talk later."

His weighted pause told me my question made him concerned about why I was calling. "Now is fine."

"I saw Helen Madison this morning."

"She came back?" he asked. "To your house or to the cafe?"

"Neither. I...um...I went to see her."

"Amy--"

Gayle Leeson

"I'm sorry. I noticed her address when you wrote it down in your notes, and I just had to know why she was so worried about Jim Normand. And I thought she'd be more open to telling me if you weren't around. I think she's afraid of the police."

"She's afraid of everyone—us, Jim Normand, Jackie." He sighed. "What did she tell you?"

"Nothing. She wouldn't even let me into her house because she was afraid she was being watched."

"Have you considered the fact that Helen Madison might simply be a drama queen?" he asked. "We deal with people like her every day who want attention."

"I know, but I don't think that's the case with her...well, at least, not entirely the case. I believe she knows something but is too scared to tell us."

"Okay, we'll talk about it over dinner. I need to get back to work."

"About dinner," I said. "What would you say to some barbecue in Brea Ridge?"

"I'd say you're trying to get us both in a lot of trouble, but since I know you well enough to know you'll go alone if I don't accompany you, I'll say that I'll pick you up at five."

"Sounds great. I love you."

"I love you, Amy."

It didn't sound like a hearts and flowers kind of declaration--more like a "what have I gotten myself into" resignation. But I'd take it.

The doorbell rang about thirty minutes before I was expecting Ryan to arrive. As Rory barked a greeting loud enough to wake the dead, I hurried to the door.

"Roger!"

"Hi, Flowerpot. Just picked this up from Dave Tucker." He indicated the large box he was carrying. "And I'd like to go ahead and install it."

"Sure, come on in." Dave Tucker was a wonderful carpenter who lived in Abingdon. I was curious to see what was in the box because Roger hadn't spoken to me about having anything made.

Rory jumped against Roger's legs as the man tried to make his way down the hall to the fancy room, which was quickly becoming a his-and-her office, thanks to Roger.

"Excuse me, Fuzz Butt," he said to Rory. "I'll have to put this box down before I can play with you."

"Come here, Rory." I picked the dog up, and he squirmed in my arms, eager to play with Roger.

When we got into the fancy room, I placed Rory onto the floor, and he hurried over to prance around Roger's feet.

Roger placed the box on the foot of my chaise and then bent to pet Rory. "Go get your ball if you want to play."

Rory raced out of the room.

Taking out a pocketknife, Roger opened the box. I could hardly wait for him to take out whatever it was inside. When he lifted it out, I could see it was a cabinet with an ornately carved door.

"Dave does exquisite work." With my fingertips, I lightly traced the shield with the lion's head in the center. "This is gorgeous. How much do I owe him?"

"Nothing." Roger grinned. "When I told him it was for you and Ryan, he made it a wedding gift."

"What? I can't let him do that!"

"That's what he said you'd say, so he told me not to tell you it was a gift."

I blinked back tears. "That's the sweetest thing ever. I'll call and thank him...and invite him to lunch."

"Maybe get this whole Helen Madison thing behind you first," he said. "You don't want to offer the guy a free meal only to have Brea Ridge's own Little Miss Nightmare run in, stand on a chair, and accuse you of poisoning people."

"Good point. Still, I don't think she'll be doing that anymore, and I need to call Dave and thank him for this masterpiece right away."

"You haven't even opened it yet," Roger said.

I opened the door to see that the deep cabinet was actually three corkboard panels with a compartment for markers, index cards, pens, tacks, and whatever else Ryan might need for his investigations.

"This is fantastic!"

"What is?" That was Ryan's voice.

I whirled to see him standing in the doorway.

"The front door was open, so I came on inside," he said.

Rory was happily tagging along at Ryan's heels.

I looked at Roger.

Shrugging, Roger said, "The gig is up, Flower-pot."

"But I wanted it to be a surprise."

Ryan looked around the room. "Amy, sweetheart, what have you done?"

"I had Roger transform my fancy room to accommodate your office."

Ryan drew in a breath. "You didn't have to do that."

"I wanted to. I know how important your office is to you."

"And I know how important this room is to you," he said.

"It still is. Even more so now." I smiled. "Do you like it?"

"I love It." He enveloped me in a hug. "I love you."

"How about me?" Roger asked. "Do you love me? I did all the work. Well, except for this—Dave Tucker did this."

Ryan inspected the cabinet. "This is amazing."

"And since you're here, you can help me hang it." Roger took the cordless drill from his toolbelt and crossed the room. "I was thinking right here. Is that okay?"

"That's great." Ryan joined Roger. "I can put my desk here, and my file cabinet in this corner, and—"

"I really wanted it to be a surprise," I repeated.

"It was, sweetheart." Ryan gave me a broad smile. "Couldn't you tell I was surprised?"

"I could," Roger said. "If I'd had a feather, I'd have knocked you over with it. I, for one, am glad the secret is out. It'll be easier to finish up the office the way you want it rather than have to go back and change things around."

"You've got a point," Ryan told him. "But before we hang this cabinet, are you sure about this, Amy?"

"I'm positive. It's my wedding present to you."

"Yeah, she's positive." Roger widened his eyes at Ryan. "I'm not putting it back the way it was."

Ryan laughed. "Thanks. I really appreciate what you've done for me."

He was looking at me, but Roger said, "You're welcome, brother."

Chapter Twenty-Three

When we arrived at the restaurant, Pete was hanging up his apron.

"Hi, Pete."

The man looked wary at my greeting and only nodded in return.

Lowering my voice, I said, "You look tired. Could I buy you a steak? Your wife could join the three of us for dinner."

Pete's eyes shifted between Ryan and me. "Don't have a wife or a girlfriend, but I won't turn down a steak dinner."

"I can drive you there and bring you back, or you can meet us there," Ryan said.

"I'll follow you in my car." Pete called goodbye to his coworkers, and the three of us went to our cars.

"Do you think he'll ditch us?" I asked Ryan, as we pulled out of the parking lot.

Ryan glanced in the rearview mirror. "I wouldn't think so. I'm not in uniform, and I'd expect Pete to be at least a little curious as to why you invited him to dinner."

"About that..." I hadn't discussed it with Ryan beforehand. "I thought he'd be more apt to talk with us if we got him away from his place of employment. Plus, by my paying for the dinner, you can't be accused of any sort of inappropriate behavior as a police officer."

He chuckled. "True. And you've always been good at getting people to talk when they have a delicious meal in front of them." Another glance in the mirror. "He's still back there. If he does decide to ditch us, though, I'll visit him in a more official capacity."

"Because you think that if he doesn't want to talk with us, he probably has something to hide?"

"Yep, especially if he passes up a free dinner."

Pete didn't ditch us. In fact, he secured the parking spot next to ours at the restaurant and walked inside with us.

We were seated, and we ordered drinks. When the server asked if we'd like an appetizer, Ryan and I deferred to Pete. He declined.

After a rather awkward wait for the server to return with our drinks and to take our orders, Pete cleared his throat. "Mind telling me what you brought me here for?"

"I want to ask you about Jim Normand," I said. "Helen Madison came to my house last night and begged me to leave the man alone."

"Have you been bothering Jim?" Pete sipped his soda, looking as if he didn't really care if I'd been bothering Jim or not.

"I didn't think so. I went around to speak with him once after having dinner at Epic Eats with some friends, but he didn't seem upset about my being there."

"Amy's cousin, Jackie, also visited Mr. Normand," Ryan said. "She can come across a bit more abrasive than Amy, so maybe she's the one who got him aggravated with the Down South Cafe staff."

"Either way, Helen seemed downright terrified." I fidgeted with my napkin. "I went to see her at her house this morning to make sure she was all right, and she would only speak with me through a crack in the door. She said she was afraid we were being watched."

Pete shrugged. "Helen is fairly high-strung."

"Are you saying you feel that she's exaggerating?" Ryan asked. "That Mr. Normand isn't someone that Helen—or Amy and her staff, for that matter— should be concerned about?"

"I wouldn't go that far." Pete drank more of his soda, either mulling over his response or hoping not to be pressed into elaborating on what he'd already said. Finally, he met Ryan's steady gaze. "Jim Normand can be a nasty piece of work. He fired Brooke and me because he needed a couple of scapegoats for that food poisoning fiasco, and he didn't give a thought as to what we were going to do."

He had emptied his glass, and the server brought him a refill.

"Jim could've avoided that entire situation by buying his mushrooms from a reputable dealer," Pete continued after the server had left the table.

"Do you believe Wood Bradford might've given Epic Eats the wrong mushrooms out of spite? Was there bad blood between the two former partners?" I asked.

"No idea." Pete spread his hands. "For the most part, Wood Bradford was a self-absorbed jerk. Sure, he could turn on the charm for the public or his customers or the television cameras or whatever; but make no mistake about it, Wood was all about Wood." He inclined his head. "And Jim is all about Jim. That's why the two of them couldn't get along. They couldn't see past themselves to the bigger picture of the business."

"Could Jim Normand, in your opinion, have had anything to do with Wood Bradford's murder?" Ryan asked.

"Who knows?" Pete shrugged. "I wouldn't put it past him, but he was already in deep trouble over the food poisoning incident. I'm not sure he'd risk retaliating against Wood when the lawyers were already breathing down his neck."

"What about Helen?" I asked. "She seems to have wanted a relationship with Mr. Bradford."

Scoffing, Pete said, "He led that poor woman around by the nose. She was handy to have around when he wanted something from her; but otherwise, she was persona non grata."

"But do you feel Helen might've had enough of Mr. Bradford's garbage and lashed out at him?" I asked.

"It's possible, but I doubt it." Looking over my left shoulder, Pete brightened. "Great! Here's our food!"

Chapter Twenty-Four

O n Thursday morning as the breakfast rush was winding down, Brooke came into the cafe. I was pouring Mr. Poston, who owns the bookstore, a second cup of coffee, and we were discussing the new books that had come in the day before.

"Good morning," Scott said to Brooke. "Welcome to the Down South Cafe. Take any free seat you'd like, and I'll be with you in a moment."

Brooke sat at the counter.

When I returned the coffee pot to its warming plate, I greeted Brooke too. "Good morning. Would you like some coffee? We have medium roast, French vanilla, and decaffeinated."

"I'd like a cup of the medium roast please." She hesitated. "And to speak with you if you have a second."

"Sure, no problem." I scanned the dining room for an empty table where we wouldn't be overheard. Then I poured her coffee, placed the cup on a saucer, and instructed her to follow me.

Scott raised his eyebrows in a silent question, and I answered him with the most minimal shrug I could manage.

I led Brooke to a table in the back right corner of the dining room. Brooke took the seat facing the dining room. I placed her coffee in front of her.

"Need sugar or cream?" I asked.

Shaking her head, she said, "It's fine as is." She glanced out the window at the parking lot.

I took the seat across from her and waited for her to speak.

At last, she said, "Pete told me that you and your boyfriend—the deputy—treated him to dinner last night."

"We did." I didn't elaborate, not sure where Brooke planned on taking the conversation.

"It was good of you to do that." She sipped her coffee. "I'm guessing you wanted to ask him some questions about Wood, but you could've done that without buying Pete dinner. He's a nice guy. I'm glad you were good to him."

"He speaks highly of you too," I said. "And he hates how you and he were let go from Epic Eats when nothing that happened regarding the food poisoning incident was your fault."

Brooke lowered her eyes. "What else did he say?"

"Basically, he told us that Wood Bradford wasn't the goody-good he tried to make himself out to be."

Snorting, she said, "You can say that again."

"Pete also told us that it was Mr. Bradford who supplied the jack-o-lantern mushrooms. I was surprised by that." I watched her face for a reaction, but Brooke was stubbornly refusing to meet my gaze. "Did he do that often? Supply the restaurant with wild mushrooms?"

"No." She took another sip of her coffee. "We typically used someone else—our regular supplier. But Jim kept complaining about the price. Wood was in the restaurant during one of Jim's rants and said he'd bring us some mushrooms on the house. That was the day before he brought the jack-o-lanterns—the day before the party."

"You're telling me that Wood Bradford provided the toxic mushrooms that were served at the family party?"

She nodded.

"Then why didn't anyone speak up and tell the truth? As far as I can tell, everyone was telling a different story about where those mushrooms came from."

Looking me in the eye at last, she said, "We didn't think it would do any good. Wood and Jim were as thick as thieves, and Wood always had the upper hand. I'm guessing he knew something about Jim that Jim preferred to keep private."

"Like what?" I asked.

She scoffed. "If I knew that, I'd still have a job."

Again, she looked down at her hands. What was she hiding?

"Brooke, do you think it's possible Jim Normand finally got fed up with Wood Bradford and murdered him?

She didn't raise her head. "How should I know?"

"Helen Madison has the idea that the mushrooms served at the party were an experiment," I said. "Why would she say that?"

When she lifted her cup this time, her hands were trembling. She raised the cup to her lips, sipped the coffee quickly, and returned the cup to the saucer. "I have no idea."

"I'm asking because Helen Madison is terrified right now," I said. "She came to my house the other night and begged me to stop bothering Mr. Normand. When I visited her at her place yesterday morning to make sure she was okay, she refused to even remove the security chain off her door and spoke to me through the crack. I tried to get her to step onto the porch so we could speak more comfortably, but she was afraid of us being seen together."

"Pete mentioned that Helen was all up in the air," Brooke said quietly. "You have to understand—Helen is strung tighter than a fiddle bow. Has been as long as I've known her."

"You're not the only person with that opinion, and I've been witness to a few of her eccentricities myself, but she's frightened of Jim Normand." I paused. "Are you?"

She shook her head. "Jim Normand did his worst to me. I'm not afraid of anything else he might do."

After Brooke left, I immediately filled Scott and Jackie in on what she'd said, and then I called Ryan.

"Why did she come to see you?" he asked. "For the sole purpose to saying she appreciated our kindness to Pete? That makes no sense."

"No, it doesn't," I agreed. "It's not like she happened to be in town and simply had an impulse to stop by—or if that was the case, she didn't say so. Besides, folks in Winter Garden generally go to Brea Ridge, not the other way around."

"Precisely. With Brea Ridge being the larger town, Winter Garden doesn't get a lot of visitors from there unless there's some sort of special event going on."

I could hear Ryan tapping his pen against his desk. He sometimes did that when he was deep in thought.

"No, she came to see you for a reason," he continued. "And I'm guessing that reason has nothing to do with Pete."

"She acted scared, but when I asked her if she—like Helen—is afraid of Jim Normand, she told me no and said he'd already done his worst to her."

"Then who—or what—is she afraid of? I'm going to talk with the sheriff and see if he concurs that we should question Brooke again. Thanks for the information, sweetheart."

"You're welcome," I said. "Be careful. I love you."

Ryan told me he loved me too, and we ended our call.

Just as Jackie and Scott moved closer to me to find out what Ryan had said about Brooke, Mom—looking weary—and Aunt Bess—looking like a racehorse champing at the bit, well, if the racehorse was wearing oversized black sunglasses—entered the cafe.

"Good morning, lovelies!" Aunt Bess pushed the sunglasses onto the top of her head. "Give us two of your finest pastries and some of that fancy vanilla coffee please."

"You've got it, beautiful," Scott said with a grin, as he walked over to the display case. "Are you feeling chocolatey or fruity this morning?"

Aunt Bess smacked her lips as if tasting an imaginary pastry. "Can't say for sure. Better give me both. I'll take a chocolate muffin and a slice of that peach pie."

"Yes, ma'am." Scott turned his attention to Mom. "Jenna?"

"I'd like a plain biscuit with butter please," she said. "And a cup of the French vanilla coffee."

I pulled her to the side. "Are you all right?"

"Aunt Bess woke me up at seven o'clock this morning eager to go on an undercover mission."

Mom hadn't lowered her voice, so Aunt Bess overheard and nodded, setting her cottony curls to bobbing.

"That's right. I'm having Jenna drive me to that Epic Eats joint to see what I can find out." She held up both hands. "No need to thank me. You young 'uns know I'm always willing to help out any way I can."

"Granny, your last undercover mission didn't go so well," Jackie reminded her. "I had to come and get you from the impound lot."

"Well, if you ask me, that was indeed a successful mission," Aunt Bess said. "We found out that Wood Bradford died, didn't we?"

"But—"

Mom shook her head. "You're wasting your breath trying to argue with her, Amy. She and I have debated the issue all morning."

"And you're actually taking Granny to do her sleuthing, Aunt Jenna?" Jackie's eyes were as wide as I imagined mine to be.

"I am," Mom said. "If I didn't, she'd simply find another way to get there. This way, I know where she is. Besides, I have some shopping to do in Brea Ridge."

"You're gonna drop Granny off at the restaurant and go shopping?" Jackie asked. "You're leaving her alone with a possible killer?"

"I don't need an amateur mucking up my investigation." Aunt Bess patted Jackie's arm, took her muffin and slice of pie, and chose a table that was bathed in sunlight.

A grinning Scott followed with her coffee.

Lowering her voice, Mom said, "I looked on the website, and Epic Eats doesn't open until noon today. It will still be closed when we get there, but we can say we tried."

Jackie and I shared a look. Neither of us thought Aunt Bess would be so easily dissuaded.

Chapter Twenty-Five

Once the lunch rush hit, I didn't have time to give any more thought to Mom and Aunt Bess. I knew Aunt Bess was a handful, but I also knew Mom had years of experience keeping her corralled. Well, at least, to the extent anyone could keep Aunt Bess under control.

Okay, let me be honest here--I had no idea what Aunt Bess might do, and I prayed she wouldn't get herself and Mom killed or arrested. But since worrying about them would've only given me frown lines, and I had food to prepare, I asked the good Lord to watch over Mom and Aunt Bess, and I concentrated on feeding our customers.

It was around two o'clock that afternoon when Mom and Aunt Bess returned to the cafe. Mom had those frown lines I'd been wanting to avoid, and I made a mental note to get her a gift certificate for the spa in Brea Ridge for Mother's Day.

Aunt Bess plopped down on a stool at the counter and told Scott, "I'll have a Diet Coke, and make it a double."

Taking a deep breath, I asked Mom, 'What happened?"

She glanced around at the still moderately populated dining room and whispered, "When the crowd thins, we'll talk. In the meantime, I'd like an iced tea."

"Make it a double?" I asked.

She nodded.

Guessing both she and Aunt Bess could also use some nourishment, I made them grilled cheese sandwiches—their go-to comfort food.

By a quarter to three, the crowd had dwindled down to a pair of older ladies who lingered over their coffee, so deep in conversation that I doubted they'd pay any attention to us whatsoever.

Moving to the end of the counter where Mom sat with Aunt Bess, I said, "All right, you two. Spill it."

"And don't leave anything out," Jackie said, coming up on my left side.

Mom waved her hand toward Aunt Bess, as if telling her she had the floor.

Never one to eschew being the center of attention, Aunt Bess leaned forward. "When we got there, Epic Eats wasn't open yet. So, we did a little shopping, milled around a little bit at the supermarket. And then, it was showtime. We went back to Epic Eats. I started out all nonchalant by going to the bathroom."

"I waited in the car," Mom said. "She convinced me that she really needed to go."

"I did!" Aunt Bess splayed her arms. "I'm not as young as I used to be, and my bladder is the size of a walnut." She frowned. "Unless that's the normal size of a bladder. Do any of y'all know how big bladders are?"

"Granny!" Jackie snapped her fingers. "Focus."

"Fine. We'll look up the bladder question later. Don't let me forget, Jenna."

Mom rolled her eyes.

Aunt Bess resumed telling her story. "So I was in the bathroom at Epic Eats, right? I was deciding the best way to approach Jim Normand when I opened the door and stepped out into the hallway. Only, guess what? Someone else had got there to interrogate the man before me." She raised her eyebrows and gave each of us a pointed look.

Obviously, she wanted someone to ask the question, so I did. "Who was it?"

"I didn't see her."

Jackie threw her hands into the air.

"But Mr. Normand called her Brooke." Aunt Bess took a drink of her soda.

"Did you hear their entire conversation?" I asked. "What were they saying?"

Now that she had us on the hook, Aunt Bess was going to keep us there as long as possible.

"I don't believe I heard everything, but I heard enough." Raising her glass in a saucy salute, she took another swig of soda.

"Granny, I swear, I'm gonna pour that drink over your head If you don't get on with this story," Jackie said.

"Fine." Aunt Bess sat her glass down, making sure to move it out of Jackie's reach. Not that she thought Jackie would actually pour the soda on her, but it paid to be cautious. "This Brooke was saying that with Wood gone now, they could pin the entire food poisoning fiasco on him—let the victims sue Wood's estate. She said—and I quote—'Whatever he had on you can't possibly matter now.'"

I wondered if Brooke's earlier visit to the cafe had prompted her to confront Jim Normand.

"And then Jim Normand said it wasn't that easy," Aunt Bess continued. "And she asked him why not, and he told her it was because the depositions had already been taken and that basically he'd done thrown her and Pete under the bus."

"How did Brooke respond to that?" I asked.

"She told him to fix it—that until the case was closed, new evidence could come to light or something. And he told her she'd seen too many lawyer shows and that he'd done paid a fortune in legal fees and couldn't afford to mount a whole new defense at this stage of the game. And then guess what she said?"

"We don't have a clue," Jackie said. "Tell us."

"She told him that if he didn't change his story and exonerate her and Pete, he'd regret it and that she'd make sure of it." Aunt Bess gave a firm nod.

"Then what happened?" I asked.

"An employee caught me standing there in the hallway between the bathroom and the dining room and asked if I was okay, so I left. I thought what I'd found out was good enough for today, and Jenna had mentioned stopping by the mall before we left Brea Ridge."

"You did great, Aunt Bess." I smiled. "Thank you."

"Anytime," she said.

I waited until after Mom and Aunt Bess had left to tell Jackie, Scott, and Luis what I planned to do.

"I'm going to go talk with Helen again," I said, as I sprayed the counter and wiped it with a cloth. "Maybe she knows what Wood Bradford had for blackmail fodder over Jim Normand. I mean, if it kept Mr. Normand from casting all the blame for the food poisoning incident on Mr. Bradford, then it must be pretty big. Right?"

Jackie, who was cleaning the door, turned. "That's a good idea. I'm going with you."

"Let me call Leslie and tell her I'll be late—"

I interrupted Scott. "There's no need for you to do that. Jackie has already said she's going, and Helen might not even be home."

"And if she is home?" Scott asked.

"She'll probably talk to us through the door again," I said.

"And we can ask her about Brooke and Pete," Jackie added. "I want to know why Normand was so eager to put all the blame for the food poisoning on them."

Luis was putting the chairs on the tables so he could mop the floor. "That's what I don't get. Why did this Normand guy have to fire two people because some of his customers got sick? Accidents happen. I mean, you wouldn't fire me if I mixed up the salt and pepper shakers, would you?"

"Of course not." I mulled over Luis's words for a moment. "Maybe Mr. Normand didn't think the food poisoning was accidental."

"Then why not blame the guy who brought the mushrooms?" Scott asked.

"Brooke thinks it's because Bradford had some dirt on Normand," Jackie said. "But is it possible Normand didn't know where the mushrooms came from? That he lashed out at the people he felt were responsible?"

"That's what we need to ask Helen." I put the cleanser beneath the counter. "That, and why she thinks the toxic mushrooms were some kind of experiment. Then if she can't or won't tell us—"

This time Scott interrupted me. "If Helen can't or won't tell you, then let the police question Mr. Normand."

"Oh, come on." Jackie stretched her back. "It's not like Normand is going to harm Amy and me in his restaurant. Besides, we still don't know for sure that he's Bradford's killer."

"All the more reason for the two of you to put away your deerstalker hats and magnifying glasses and do something fun this afternoon." Scott grinned. "You're becoming more like Aunt Bess by the day."

He and Luis laughed over our protests. As much as I hated to admit it, maybe we were becoming like Aunt Bess—seeking adventure, wanting to solve crimes.

But we had to this time. The reputation of the Down South Cafe was on the line.

Right?

Chapter Twenty-Six

As soon as we'd finished tidying the cafe, Jackie and I left Scott and Luis to lock up. We hopped into my bright yellow Bug—nothing like being inconspicuous—and headed toward Helen Madison's house.

"Do you believe she'll open the door more than a crack this time?" Jackie asked.

"I highly doubt it." I gave the matter some thought. "If I park the Bug a street over, then she might be more receptive to letting us in."

"Amy, she'll still recognize us as soon as she looks outside."

"True, but she acted nervous when she thought someone could drive by and see me there. She might be more likely to allow us to go inside out of sight if the Bug isn't parked outside her house."

When we reached Helen's street, it wasn't as easy as I'd hoped to find a place to park that still wasn't too close to her house. We wound up leaving the Bug at the back of the Brea Ridge Elementary School parking lot and walking about a quarter of a mile to Helen's house.

Jackie and I glanced at each other warily before stepping onto Helen's porch.

"Do you want to do the honors or shall I?" I asked softly.

"You'd better take the lead. She might think I'm here to smush more of her bread."

"To be honest, I wouldn't put it past you."

She shrugged. "I'm trying to control myself, but I can't make any promises."

Jackie stepped out of sight of the keyhole as I knocked on Helen's door. Given their history, I thought that was a good move. Helen might not be pleased to see me, but she'd be even less inclined to open the door if she saw Jackie with me.

"Helen, it's Amy Flowers! I have a quick question for you!"

"Please go away. I have nothing more to say to you." Her voice was slightly muffled but clear enough that I could tell she was just on the other side of the door.

"It's only one question," I insisted. "I parked at the elementary school and walked here so no one would see my car."

Flinging open the door, she said, "Fine, make it fast." Then she spotted Jackie. "You! What're you doing here?"

Helen would've stepped back into her house and slammed the door, but Jackie lunged forward fast enough to wedge herself between the woman and the door.

"We're not here to bother you or to demolish your bread," Jackie said. "Answer our question, and we'll be on our way. What blackmail information did Wood Bradford have on Jim Normand?"

Helen frowned. "Blackmail? Wood was blackmailing Jim?"

"Was he?" I asked.

"Not that I know of," Helen said. "Why would he do that?"

"Brooke thinks Mr. Bradford must've had some damning evidence on Mr. Normand to keep Mr. Normand from placing the blame for the toxic mushrooms on Mr. Bradford," I said.

Shaking her head, Helen's said, "Wood wouldn't have known a morel from a magpie. He had nothing to do with those mushrooms."

I felt a sharp sting in my left shoulder and looked around to see if I'd been stung by a bee. Seeing a red laser dot on Jackie's face, I shoved my cousin aside shouting, "Get down! Somebody's shooting at us!"

Jackie pushed Helen out of the way, put her arm around me, and muscled us both into Helen's house. Then she jerked Helen backward and slammed the door.

"Lock that door and get down."

Helen did as Jackie had instructed.

"I've been hit," I told Jackie. "On my shoulder." I slumped to the floor. "It doesn't hurt as much as I'd have thought it would. Maybe that's the adrenaline, I don't know."

"Let me see." Jackie gingerly leaned me forward.

I was aware of Helen moving closer for a better look at my wound.

A shot to the shoulder wasn't good, of course, but it wasn't fatal...unless the bullet nicked an artery or something.

"Do you bleed yellow?" Helen asked.

"No, she doesn't bleed yellow," Jackie said. "Do you think she's an alien or something? Call the police

and tell them someone is shooting at us with a paintball gun."

"A paintball gun?" I breathed a sigh of relief. "Oh,
thank goodness."

"Yes, it's much less worrisome, but the fact re-
mains that someone is out there trying to hurt us or
at least scare us, and I'm not having it." Jackie stood.

"You can't go after this person," I said. "What if
they have a weapon other than a paintball gun?"

"I'll call the police right now," Helen added, cross-
ing the room to get her phone.

"By the time they get here, whoever it is could be
gone." Jackie looked at Helen. "Do you have any sort
of weapon?"

"Not really."

Not willing to accept no for an answer, Jackie
sprang over to the dining room table and grabbed a
long-handled charcuterie board and a tall glass candlestick. "These will have to do." She handed the
candlestick to me. "Use this to protect yourself if the
attacker should get in here somehow."

"As if." I got to my feet. "I'm going with you."

Jackie nodded. "Let's go."

"Don't y'all break my stuff!" Helen yelled, as Jackie and I barreled out the front door.

As soon as she placed a foot on the porch, Jackie was hit on the leg with a blob of yellow paint. Raising the charcuterie board above her head and giving a war cry, she took off running. I gripped the candlestick and sprinted behind her.

I heard three consecutive thump-thump-thumps of the paintball gun firing before spotting Brooke rise up out of her hiding spot across from Helen's house.

Brooke ran, but she was no match for Jackie, who tackled her with a vengeance. I was seconds behind Jackie, and the Brea Ridge police officers—sirens blaring—were seconds behind me.

As Jackie let Brooke get up, a booming voice instructed all of us to stay where we were and to put our hands in the air. Jackie and I immediately complied.

"I can't raise my hands!" Brooke shouted. "She broke my shoulder!"

"It's not broken—only dislocated." Jackie rolled her eyes. "Want me to pop it back into place, you big baby?"

"No! Don't touch her." The booming voice moved closer. "You need to tell me what's going on here, one at a time."

Naturally, we all started speaking at once. The booming voice, which belonged to a middle-aged officer who didn't appear inclined to put up with a lot of nonsense, shushed us.

Then he turned to Helen, who stood a few yards away from us wringing her hands. "You. Are you the homeowner who made the 9-1-1 call?"

"Y-yes, sir. I-I just want her to stop. I want to be left alone."

"Helen, I'm sorry I bothered you," I said. "I was--"

"Not you," Helen interrupted. "Her! I want Brooke to leave me alone!"

"You'd better shut up." Brooke took a step toward Helen. "Don't you dare say another word."

Booming Voice did not appreciate Brooke's interference. "You are not in charge here. Back up to where you were standing before and don't move again."

Brooke stepped back but continued glaring at Helen.

Booming Voice spoke into the radio clipped to his right shoulder and instructed dispatch to send backup. "I'm gonna have to bring these four women into the station for questioning."

I sighed. Why hadn't we listened to Scott?

The Brea Ridge police station looked a lot like the Winter Garden police station. There were lots of desks and police officers, uniformed and plain clothes, and the smell of burning coffee hung in the air.

We hadn't been handcuffed, which was nice, but we had been placed in the back of four separate police cars because the officers were afraid that if they put us together, we might kill each other. It was a valid argument. Besides the combination of Jackie and me, I couldn't guarantee there wouldn't have been a violent altercation among us. I didn't especially feel like punching Helen, but I couldn't speak for Jackie; and we'd both probably be willing to take a shot at Brooke—and vice versa. And Brooke seemed to want to murder us all.

Imagine my surprise—and relief—when Sheriff Billings walked through the door...followed by Ryan—my precious Ryan. And Roger.

Roger? What's he doing here?

None of the men looked happy to be here.

I glanced at Jackie—always ready for a fight—lifting her chin.

Booming Voice, who we now knew to be Sergeant Harcourt, led me, Jackie, and the men from Winter Garden into an interview room and asked us to take seats.

Starting with Jackie, he asked what had taken place that afternoon. She gave him all of the facts without candy-coating anything.

When Jackie had finished giving her account of the events that had led to our visit to the Brea Ridge Police Department, Sergeant Harcourt turned to me. "Do you concur with Ms. Fonseca's testimony as to what occurred?"

"Yes, sir."

"Do you have anything to add?" he asked.

"No, sir."

Sergeant Harcourt explained that Jackie and I would normally have been questioned separately, but since there were no pending charges and because Sheriff Billings had vouched for us, he expedited the time spent obtaining the facts from us.

"Also, Helen Madison is singing like a sparrow in the interview room next door," he said. "The woman who had the paintball gun has been harassing her ever since the death of Woodrow Bradford." He nodded at Sheriff Billings. "I think we're good here. If you and your deputies would like to question Ms. Madison, you may join the officer in Interview Room Two. Brooke Shipley is receiving medical care, but she'll be at your disposal when she arrives."

The sergeant once again turned his attention to Jackie and me. "If you want to file assault charges against Brooke Shipley, see the magistrate on your way out. Otherwise, you're free to go."

We all filed out of the room.

Ryan fell back and placed his hand on the small of my back. "You all right, sweetheart?" he asked softly.

I nodded.

"We'll probably be late here, but I'll see you as soon as I can—either tonight or tomorrow." He winked.

"Thank you."

Putting his professional mask back in place, he nodded and joined Sheriff Billings and Sergeant Harcourt.

"I'm here to drive you back to your cars," Roger said.

"Let's go," Jackie said. "I'm eager to get home and get changed."

On the way to the parking lot where I'd left the Bug, Roger explained that Scott had called Ivy not long after Jackie and I had left the cafe. He'd told her that given Helen's erratic behavior in the past, he was concerned about our visiting her.

"Scott told Ivy that Helen had made it crystal clear that she was frightened and wanted nothing to do with the two of you," Roger said. "Ivy agreed that you shouldn't have gone. In fact, Ivy was on her way to intercept you when she heard the call come over the radio and alerted Sheriff Billings. He told her he and Ryan would handle the matter. En route, Ryan called and asked me to meet them in Brea Ridge."

"That explains how Sheriff Billings and Ryan got to the police station not long after we did," I said.

"Jackie, other than looking like a Jackson Pollock painting, are you okay?" Roger asked.

"Yeah. I'm just thinking about something Sergeant Harcourt said." She turned in her seat to frown at me. "He said Helen told the police that Brooke had been tormenting her ever since Wood Bradford's death. Could it be Brooke, rather than Jim Normand, who Helen feared?"

"Well, Helen did beg me to leave Jim Normand alone," I said. "She didn't specify that he had threatened her or told her he'd harm her if we didn't stop bothering him. But why would Brooke care about our talking to Jim Normand?"

"Maybe he's her love bug." Roger elbowed Jackie playfully as he made the joke.

"Maybe he is," I said. "Or was." And I wasn't joking.

I texted Ryan: *Ask Brooke about her relationship with Jim Normand. Was she the one who warned Helen that there would be trouble if we didn't leave Normand alone?*

"Texting your love bug, Flowerpot?" Roger teased.

"Yeah. Knowing the lengths Brooke would go to in order to scare us away from Helen's house and the fact that she lied about Wood Bradford providing the toxic mushrooms, some of the puzzle pieces are starting to fall into place."

"At least, they've got her now," Jackie said. "That's the main thing."

"Yeah, I hope they can keep her."

"You think she killed Bradford, don't you?" Roger asked.

"I do."

The parking lot of the elementary school was packed when we arrived. There must have been some sporting event or play or something going on. Roger parked his truck in front of the Bug, and I climbed out.

"I was planning to drive Jackie to the cafe to get her car, but if you're too shaken up to drive, we can call—"

Waving my hand, I said, "Nah. I'm fine."

"Okay. We'll be right behind you," he said.

"Since I'll need you to move before I can pull out, I'll be right behind you," I said with a smile.

"Stay close, Flowerpot. We want to be able to see your Bug eyes all the way home."

"Aye, aye, Captain." Giving Roger a mocking salute and Jackie a wave, I unlocked the Bug and got in. It felt like going home to be in my comfy little car after the ordeal I'd been through.

Roger waited to make sure the car would start, and then he slowly pulled out of the parking lot. I put the car in drive and followed the truck down the road.

The road was curvy, and it wasn't possible to keep the truck's taillights in view for the entire drive. That's one reason I became nervous when my headlights began flickering. I went into a full-blown panic when my car stalled completely.

I turned on my four-way flashers, but they failed after a few seconds. The interior light wouldn't come on either. I knew it must be a problem with my battery but knowing that information didn't help me right now. I had to get the car out of the road before I got hit.

While I was fumbling through my purse for my phone, I was startled by a rap on the driver's side window. Turning, I expected to see Roger. Instead, I saw Ruthie Shipley, Brooke's daughter. What were the odds?

She was smiling. "Having trouble?"

"Yes. I'm going to call my friend Roger to come help me." I kept searching for my phone.

"Before you call anyone, we need to get your car out of the middle of the road," she said. "I've got mine blocking traffic at the moment, but we'll both be hurting if somebody comes barreling around that curve."

"True."

"If you can put it into neutral, I believe the two of us can get it to the side of the road and call a tow truck." Ruthie was still smiling.

I knew she was right about our needing to get the cars out of the road, but I didn't trust her. Had she heard from Brooke? Did she know what had taken place at Helen's house? There was something eerie behind that smile.

Nevertheless, I put the car in neutral and opened the door. "Can you push while I steer?"

"No problem."

She was as good as her word—at least, on that point--and the two of us managed to maneuver the Bug to the shoulder of the road.

"Thanks so much," I told her. "I'll call my friends now to come back and get me. No need for you to wait."

"Nonsense." Ruthie looked back at her car and jerked her head.

It was then that I realized there was someone else in the car. And that person was driving the car.

"We wouldn't dream of leaving you out here on your own," Ruthie said.

"We?"

"Mom and I. I picked her up from the hospital."

I tried to shut the car door, but Ruthie caught it. "Don't be ungrateful. Mom wants to say hi."

Brooke drove the car and parked it behind mine. She got out and walked toward us. Her injured arm was in a sling. I made a mental note to use that injury to my advantage if I had to fight dirty. Still, it was two against one, and I didn't like those odds.

Standing beside her daughter, Brooke asked me, "You think you're clever, don't you?"

"I'm not as clever as you," I said. "How did you ditch the officer who was with you at the hospital?"

"That wasn't hard. Just slipped out when no one was looking. Had them all fooled into thinking I was the victim." She indicated her arm. "Which I am."

"Why'd you kill Wood Bradford?" I asked.

"Who said I did?"

"I don't know." I shrugged. "Just if you did, that was the epitome of clever."

Brooke squinted at me. "What do you mean by that?"

"Well, you had the police suspecting me and my staff, Helen, Jim Normand, even Janine from the post office." I paused. "My best guess is that you were trying to frame Jim because he fired you."

"Jim is an idiot." Brooke spat out the words as if they tasted bad. "I loved that man. Waited for him to see me, to settle down with me. Watched Wood Bradford take advantage of Jim again and again. Those jack-o-lantern mushrooms were a test."

"Mom." Ruthie's voice held a warning.

Brooke kept talking. "I wanted to see just how toxic they were. Turned out, they weren't toxic enough. I had to rely on antifreeze in Wood's coffee thermos. The idiot didn't even question it when I offered to make him some fresh coffee."

"Mom. Shut. Up."

Turning on her daughter, Brooke said, "Why don't *you* shut up? Anything she says is her word against ours. No one is going to believe her."

Still afraid that Brooke intended to kill me, I said, "For what it's worth, I'm sorry for what Mr. Bradford did to you and Mr. Normand. And Mr. Normand was foolish if he didn't appreciate you."

"Yeah, right."

Brooke's words were drowned out by Roger's truck roaring around the curve. The truck swerved sideways, blocking both lanes of traffic. The four-way flashers turned on before Roger and Jackie leapt from the truck and attacked Brooke and Ruthie.

"Thank goodness!" I said, as I got out of the car. I looked around to see who to help, but Roger and Jackie had Ruthie and Brooke pinned to the ground, respectively. "I'll call for backup."

Chapter Twenty-Seven

Home had never felt so good when I got there at last. Both Rory and Princess Eloise came to love on me—of course, they were hungry, and Princess Eloise went right to Ryan after rubbing against my ankles—and I was struck with how very wonderful my little house was.

"I'm really glad you want to live here," I said to Ryan after we'd gotten the pets fed and cuddled up on the sofa.

"Just feels like home," he said, with a tired smile.

The five of us—Sheriff Billings, Jackie, Roger, Ryan, and I--had agreed not to mention anything about the evening's events to Mom and Aunt Bess until tomorrow...after work. Aunt Bess would be fit to be tied, and she'd want photographs of the Bug to add to her Crime Scenes Pinterest board, but she'd be all right. We'd make her a special cake or something to soften the blow.

As Ryan and I sat there holding each other, I reflected on what a night we'd had.

While Brooke and Ruthie were sabotaging my car and cornering me on the side of the road, Helen had been telling Sergeant Harcourt and Sheriff Billings how Brooke had been threatening her ever since Wood Bradford's death. Brooke had told Helen to put the blame on the cafe, and to make a big show of accusing us of poisoning the man.

Helen certainly had done her part there.

Then, when the police didn't take Helen's accusations against the cafe seriously, Brooke began throwing suspicion onto Helen and Janine. She drew the line at any hint of impropriety against Jim Normand, however, and when we began questioning him, Brooke really started to spiral. She had Helen warn us to leave Mr. Normand alone...or else. Seeing how unhinged Brooke had become, Helen was terrified. She'd begun to suspect that Brooke had killed Mr. Bradford and was afraid she'd kill her too.

Brooke didn't say much until she was presented with Helen's testimony, my testimony, and the evidence procured against her by the Winter Garden Sheriff's Office. Our officers were absolutely wonderful at their jobs. They seldom needed assistance from civilians, but some civilians were willing to help out all the same.

Ruthie confessed to tampering with my battery cable to make my car stall. She was friends with a locksmith who unlocked the car for her. I supposed I was lucky my car didn't catch fire or that I didn't wreck when it stalled.

With Brooke admitting she knew the mushrooms were toxic and served them anyway, I supposed Billy Hancock would file a motion to dismiss the case against Epic Eats. While the restaurant likely still bore some responsibility for the food poisoning, the family would probably be willing to settle out of court and see that charges were filed against Brooke for willingly poisoning them.

Whatever the case may be, I wasn't worried about any of it. I was fine. Jackie was fine. The cafe's reputation was intact. And I had a wedding to plan.

"What are you smiling about?" Ryan asked, kissing my forehead.

"I'm thinking about our wedding. And I believe I know just where to get my dress."

Recipes from the Down South Café

Chocolate Caramel Coffee Pretzel Bars:

https://www.delish.com/cooking/recipe-ideas/a62157517/chocolate-caramel-coffee-pretzel-bars-recipe/

Carrot Souffle:

https://www.allrecipes.com/recipe/21463/carrot-souffle/

Apple Butter Pizza:

https://www.askchefdennis.com/a-taste-of-fall-with-my-apple-butter-pizza/

*If you like these recipes (and not just links!), check out *Tea For You*, a complimentary e-book of recipes based on the Victoria Square Mysteries and the Life On Victoria Square companion series which I co-write with Lorraine Bartlett. To download the e-book, visit me at http://www.gayleleeson.com and click the *Victoria Square Series* tab.

Also by Gayle Leeson

Down South Café Mystery Series
The Calamity Café

Silence of the Jams

Honey-Baked Homicide

Apples and Alibis

Fruit Baskets and Holiday Caskets

Truffles and Tragedy

Pickled to Death

Cake and I Scream

Ghostly Fashionista Mystery Series
Designs on Murder

Perils and Lace

Christmas Cloches and Corpses

Buttons and Blows

Secrets and Sequins

Corsets and Casualties

Kinsey Falls Women's Fiction Series
Hightail It to Kinsey Falls

Putting Down Roots in Kinsey Falls

Sleighing It in Kinsey Falls

Victoria Square Series (With Lorraine Bartlett)

Yule Be Dead

Murder Ink

Murderous Misconception

Embroidery Mystery Series (Written as Amanda Lee)

The Quick and The Thread

Stitch Me Deadly

Thread Reckoning

The Long Stitch Goodnight

Thread on Arrival

Cross-Stitch Before Dying

Thread End

Wicked Stitch

The Stitching Hour

Better Off Thread

Cake Decorating Mystery Series (Written as Gayle Trent)

Murder Takes the Cake

Dead Pan

Killer Sweet Tooth

Battered to Death

Killer Wedding Cake

Myrtle Crumb Mystery Series (Written as Gayle Trent)

The Party Line (short story/prequel)

Between A Clutch and a Hard Place

When Good Bras Go Bad

Claus of Death

Soup...Er...Myrtle!

Perp and Circumstance

ABOUT THE AUTHOR

Gayle Leeson is known for her cozy mysteries. She also writes as Gayle Trent and Amanda Lee. To eliminate confusion going forward, Gayle is writing under the name Gayle Leeson only. She and her family live in Southwest Virginia with Cooper, the Great Pyrenees in the photograph with Gayle, and a small pride of lions (cats, really, but humor them).

If you enjoyed this book, Gayle would appreciate your leaving a review. If you don't know what to say,

there is a handy book review guide at her site (https://www.gayleleeson.com/book-review-form). Gayle invites you to sign up for her newsletter and receive excerpts of some of her books:
https://forms.aweber.com/form/14/1780369214.htm

Social Media Links:
Twitter:

https://twitter.com/GayleTrent

Facebook:

https://www.facebook.com/GayleLeeson/

BookBub:

https://www.bookbub.com/profile/gayle-leeson

Goodreads:

https://www.goodreads.com/author/show/426208.Gayle_Trent

Have You Met Max, the Ghostly Fashionista?

Excerpt from *Designs on Murder*

Chapter One

A flash of brilliant light burst from the lower righthand window of Shops on Main, drawing my attention to the FOR LEASE sign. I'd always loved the building and couldn't resist going inside to see the space available.

I opened the front door to the charming old mansion, which had started life as a private home in the late 1800s and had had many incarnations since then. I turned right to open another door to go into the vacant office.

"Why so glum, chum?" asked a tall, attractive woman with a dark brown bob and an impish grin. She stood near the window wearing a rather fancy mauve gown for the middle of the day. She was also wearing a headband with a peacock feather, making her look like a flapper from the 1920s. I wondered if she might be going to some sort of party after work. Either that, or this woman was quite the eccentric.

"I just came from a job interview," I said.

"Ah. Don't think it went well, huh?"

"Actually, I think it did. But I'm not sure I want to be doing that kind of work for...well...forever."

"Nothing's forever, darling. But you've come to the right place. My name's Max, by the way. Maxine, actually, but I hate that stuffy old name. Maxine Englebright. Isn't that a mouthful? You can see why I prefer Max."

I chuckled. "It's nice to meet you, Max. I'm Amanda Tucker."

"So, Amanda Tucker," Max said, moving over to the middle of the room, "what's your dream job?"

"I know it'll sound stupid. I shouldn't have even wandered in here--"

"Stop that please. Negativity gets us nowhere."

Max sounded like a school teacher then, and I tried to assess her age. Although she somehow seemed older, she didn't look much more than my twenty-four years. I'd put her at about thirty...if that. Since she was looking at me expectantly, I tried to give a better answer to her question.

"I want to fill a niche...to make some sort of difference," I said. "I want to do something fun, exciting...something I'd look forward to doing every day."

"And you're considering starting your own business?"

"That was my initial thought upon seeing that this space is for lease. I love this building...always have."

"What sort of business are you thinking you'd like to put here?" Max asked.

"I enjoy fashion design, but my parents discouraged me because—they said—it was as hard to break into as professional sports. I told them there are a lot of people in professional sports, but they said, 'Only the best, Mandy.'"

Max gave an indignant little bark. "Oh, that's hooey! But I can identify. My folks never thought I'd amount to much. Come to think of it, I guess I didn't." She threw back her head and laughed.

"Oh, well, I wish I could see some of your designs."

"You can. I have a couple of my latest right here on my phone." I took my cell phone from my purse and pulled up the two designs I'd photographed the day before. The first dress had a small pink and green floral print on a navy background, shawl collar, three-quarter length sleeves, and A-line skirt. "I love vintage styles."

"This is gorgeous! I'd love to have a dress like this."

"Really?"

"Yeah. What else ya got?" Max asked.

My other design was an emerald 1930s-style bias cut evening gown with a plunging halter neckline and a back panel with pearl buttons that began at the middle of the back on each side and went to the waist.

Max caught her breath. "That's the berries, kid!"

"Thanks." I could feel the color rising in my cheeks. Max might throw out some odd phrases, but I could tell she liked the dress. "Mom and Dad are probably right, though. Despite the fact that I use modern fabrics—some with quirky, unusual patterns—how could I be sure I'd have the clientele to actually support a business?"

"Are you kidding me? People would love to have their very own fashion designer here in little ol' Abingdon."

"You really think so? Is it the kind of place you'd visit?" I asked.

"Visit?" Max laughed. "Darling, I'd practically live in it."

"All right. I'll think about it."

"Think quickly please. There was someone in here earlier today looking at the space. He wants to sell cigars and tobacco products. Pew. The smell would drive me screwy. I'd much rather have you here."

Hmm...the lady had her sales pitch down. I had to give her that. "How much is the rent?"

"Oh, I have no idea. You'll find Mrs. Meacham at the top of the stairs, last door on your left. It's marked OFFICE."

"Okay. I'll go up and talk with her."

"Good luck, buttercup!"

I was smiling and shaking my head as I mounted the stairs. Max was a character. I thought she'd be a fun person to have around.

Since the office wasn't a retail space like the other rooms in the building, I knocked and waited for a response before entering.

Mrs. Meacham was a plump, prim woman with short, curly white hair and sharp blue eyes. She looked at me over the top of her reading glasses. "How may I help you?"

"I'm interested in the space for rent downstairs," I said.

"You are? Oh, my! I thought you were here selling cookies or something. You look so young." Mrs. Meacham laughed at her own joke, so I faked a chortle to be polite. "What type of shop are you considering?"

"A fashion boutique."

"Fashion?"

"Yes, I design and create retro-style fashions."

"Hmm. I never picked up sewing myself. I've never been big on crafts." She stood and opened a file cabinet to the left of her desk, and I could see she was wearing a navy suit. "Canning and baking were more my strengths. I suppose you could say I prefer the kitchen to the hearth." She laughed again, and I chuckled along with her.

She turned and handed me an application. "Just read this over and call me back if you have any questions. If you're interested in the space, please let me know as soon as possible. There's a gentleman interested in opening a cigar store there." She tapped a pen on her desk blotter. "But even if he gets here before you do, we'll have another opening by the first of the month. The web designer across the hall is leaving. Would you like to take a look at his place before you decide?"

"No, I'd really prefer the shop on the ground floor," I said.

"All right. Well, I hope to hear from you soon."

I left then. I stopped back by the space for lease to say goodbye to Max, but she was gone.

I went home—my parents' home actually, but they moved to Florida for Dad's job more than two years ago, so it was basically mine...until they wanted it back. I made popcorn for lunch, read over Mrs. Meacham's contract, and started crunching the numbers.

I'd graduated in May with a bachelor's degree in business administration with a concentration in marketing and entrepreneurship but just couldn't find a position that sparked any sort of passion in me.

This morning I'd had yet another interview where I'd been overqualified for the position but felt I had a good chance of getting an offer...a low offer...for work I couldn't see myself investing decades doing.

Jasmine, my cat, wandered into the room. She'd eaten some kibble from her bowl in the kitchen and was now interested in what I was having. She hopped onto the coffee table, peeped into the popcorn bowl, and turned away dismissively to clean her paws. She was a beautiful gray and white striped tabby. Her feet were white, and she looked as if she were wearing socks of varying lengths—crew socks on the back, anklets on the front.

"What do you think, Jazzy?" I asked. "Should I open a fashion boutique?"

She looked over her shoulder at me for a second before resuming her paw-licking. I didn't know if that was a yes or a no.

Even though I'd gone to school for four years to learn all about how to open, manage, and provide inventory for a small business, I researched for the remainder of the afternoon. I checked out the stats on independent designers in the United States and fashion boutiques in Virginia. There weren't many in the Southwest Virginia region, so I knew I'd have something unique to offer my clientele.

Finally, Jazzy let me know that she'd been napping long enough and that we needed to do something. Mainly, I needed to feed her again, and she wanted to eat. But I had other ideas.

"Jazzy, let's get your carrier. You and I are going to see Grandpa Dave."

Grandpa Dave was my favorite person on the planet, and Jazzy thought pretty highly of him herself. He lived only about ten minutes away from us. He was farther out in the country and had a bigger home than we did. Jazzy and I were happy in our little three-bedroom, one bath ranch. We secretly hoped Dad wouldn't lose the job that had taken him and Mom to Florida and that they'd love it too much to leave when he retired because we'd gotten used to having the extra space.

I put the carrier on the backseat of my green sedan. It was a cute car that I'd worked the summer between high school and college to get enough money to make the down payment on, but it felt kinda ironic to be driving a cat around in a car that reminded people of a hamster cage.

Sometimes, I wished my Mom and Dad's house was a bit farther from town. It was so peaceful out here in the country. Fences, pastureland, and cows bordered each side of the road. There were a few houses here and there, but most of the land was still farmland. The farmhouses were back off the road and closer to the barns.

When we pulled into Grandpa Dave's long driveway, Jazzy meowed.

"Yes," I told her. "We're here."

Grandpa Dave lived about fifty yards off the road, and his property was fenced, but he didn't keep any animals. He'd turned the barn that had been on the land when he and Grandma Jodie bought it into a workshop where he liked to "piddle."

I pulled around to the side of the house and was happy to see that, rather than piddling in the workshop, Grandpa was sitting on one of the white rocking chairs on the porch. I parked and got out, opened the door to both the car and the carrier for Jazzy, and she ran straight to hop onto his lap.

"Well, there's my girls!" Grandpa Dave laughed.

It seemed to me that Grandpa was almost always laughing. He'd lost a little of that laughter after Grandma Jodie had died. But that was five years ago, and, except for some moments of misty remembrance, he was back to his old self.

I gave him a hug and a kiss on the cheek before settling onto the swing.

"I was sorta expecting you today," he said. "How'd the interview go?"

"It went fine, I guess, but I'm not sure Integrated Manufacturing Technologies is for me. The boss was nice, and the offices are beautiful, but...I don't know."

"What ain't she telling me, Jazzy?"

The cat looked up at him adoringly before butting her head against his chin.

"I'm...um...I'm thinking about starting my own business." I didn't venture a glance at Grandpa Dave right away. I wasn't sure I wanted to know what he was thinking. I figured he was thinking I'd come to ask for money--which I had, money and advice—but I was emphatic it was going to be a loan.

Grandpa had already insisted on paying my college tuition and wouldn't hear of my paying him back. This time, I was giving him no choice in the matter. Either he'd lend me the money, and sign the loan agreement I'd drafted, or I wouldn't take it.

I finally raised my eyes to look at his face, and he was looking pensive.

"Tell me what brought this on," he said.

I told him about wandering into Shops on Main after my interview and meeting Maxine Englebright. "She loved the designs I showed her and seemed to think I could do well if I opened a boutique there. I went upstairs and got an application from the building manager, and then I went home and did some research. I'd never seriously considered opening my own business before--at least, not at this stage of my career--but I'd like to try."

Another glance at Grandpa Dave told me he was still listening but might take more convincing.

"I realize I'm young, and I'm aware that more than half of all small businesses fail in the first four years. But I've got a degree that says I'm qualified to manage a business. Why not manage my own?"

He remained quiet.

"I know that opening a fashion boutique might seem frivolous, but there aren't a lot of designers in this region. I believe I could fill a need...or at least a niche."

Grandpa sat Jazzy onto the porch and stood. Without a word, he went into the house.

Jazzy looked up at me. *Meow?* She went over to the door to see where Grandpa Dave went. *Meow?* She stood on her hind legs and peered through the door.

"Watch out, Jasmine," he said, waiting for her to hop down and back away before he opened the door.

He was carrying his checkbook. "How much do you need?"

"Well, I have some savings, and—"

"That's not what I asked."

"Okay. Now, this will be a loan, Grandpa Dave, not a gift."

"If you don't tell me how much, I'm taking this checkbook back into the house, and we won't discuss it any further."

"Ten thousand dollars," I blurted.

As he was writing the check, he asked, "Have you and Jazzy had your dinner yet?"

We were such frequent guests that he kept her favorite cat food on hand.

"We haven't. Do you have the ingredients to make a pizza?"

He scoffed. "Like I'm ever without pizza-makings." He handed me the check. "By the way, how old is this Max you met today? She sounds like quite a gal."

"She doesn't look all that much older than me. But she seems more worldly...or something. I think you'd like her," I said. "But wait, aren't you still seeing Betsy?"

He shrugged. "Betsy is all right to take to Bingo...but this Max sounds like she could be someone special."

First thing the next morning, I went to the bank to set up a business account for Designs on You. That's what I decided to name my shop. Then I went to Shops on Main and gave Mrs. Meacham my application. After she made sure everything was in order, she took my check for the first month's rent and then took me around to meet the rest of the shop owners.

She introduced me to the upstairs tenants first. There was Janice, who owned Janice's Jewelry. She was of average height but she wore stilettos, had tawny hair with blonde highlights, wore a shirt that was way too tight, and was a big fan of dermal fillers, given her expressionless face.

"Janice, I'd like you to meet Amanda," said Mrs. Meacham. "She's going to be opening a fashion boutique downstairs."

"Fashion? You and I should talk, Amanda. You dress them, and I'll accessorize them." She giggled before turning to pick up a pendant with a large, light green stone. "With your coloring, you'd look lovely in one of these Amazonite necklace and earring sets."

"I'll have to check them out later," I said. "It was nice meeting you."

Janice grabbed a stack of her business cards and pressed them into my hand. "Here. For your clients. I'll be glad to return the favor."

"Great. Thanks."

Next, Mrs. Meacham took me to meet Mark, a web site designer. Everything about Mark screamed thin. The young man didn't appear to have an ounce of fat on his body. He had thinning black hair. He wore a thin crocheted tie. He held out a thin hand for me to shake. His handshake was surprisingly firm.

"Hello. It's a pleasure to meet you, Amanda." He handed me a card from the holder on his desk. "Should you need any web design help or marketing expertise, please call on me. I can work on a flat fee or monthly fee basis, depending on your needs."

"Thank you, but—"

"Are you aware that fifty percent of fledgling businesses fail within the first year?" he asked.

I started to correct his stats, but I didn't want to alienate someone I was going to be working near. I thanked him again and told him I appreciated his offer. It dawned on me as Mrs. Meacham and I were moving on to the next tenant that she'd said the web designer was leaving at the end of the month...which was only a week away. I wondered where he was taking his business.

The other upstairs shop was a bookstore called Antiquated Editions. The owner was a burly, bearded man who'd have looked more at home in a motor-cycle shop than selling rare books, but, hey, you can't judge a book by its cover, right?

I made a mental note to tell Grandpa Dave my little joke. As you've probably guessed, I didn't have a lot of friends. Not that I wasn't a friendly person. I had a lot of acquaintances. It was just hard for me to get close to people. I wasn't the type to tell my deepest, darkest secrets to someone I hadn't known...well, all my life.

The brawny book man's name was Ford. I'd have been truly delighted had it been Harley, but had you been expecting me to say his name was Fitzgerald or Melville, please see the aforementioned joke about books and covers. He was friendly and invited me to come around and look at his collection anytime. I promised I'd do so after I got settled in.

Then it was downstairs to meet the rest of the shop owners. The first shop on the left when you came in the door--the shop directly across the hall from mine--was Delightful Home. The proprietress was Connie, who preferred a hug over a handshake.

"Aren't you lovely?" Connie asked.

I did not say I doubt it, which was the first thought that popped into my brain, but I did thank her for the compliment. Connie was herself the embodiment of lovely. She had long, honey blonde hair that she wore in a single braid. Large silver hoops adorned her ears, and she had skinny silver bracelets stacked up each arm. She wore an embroidered red tunic that fell to her thighs, black leggings, and Birkenstocks. But the thing that made her truly lovely wasn't so much her looks but the way she appeared to boldly embrace life. I mean, the instant we met, she embraced me. Her shop smelled of cinnamon and something else...sage, maybe.

"Melba, that blue is definitely your color," Connie said. "By the way, did that sinus blend help you?"

"It did!" Mrs. Meacham turned to me. "Connie has the most wonderful products, not the least of which are her essential oils."

I could see that Connie had an assortment of candles, soaps, lotions, oils, and tea blends. I was curious to see what all she did have, but that would have to wait.

"I'm here to help you in any way I possibly can," said Connie, with a warm smile. "Anything you need, just let me know. We're neighbors now."

Mrs. Meacham took me to meet the last of my "neighbors," Mr. and Mrs. Peterman.

"Call us Ella and Frank," Ella insisted. She was petite with salt-and-pepper hair styled in a pixie cut.

Frank was average height, had a slight paunch, a bulbous nose, and bushy brown hair. He didn't say much.

Ella and Frank had a paper shop. They designed their own greeting cards and stationery, and they sold specialty and novelty items that would appeal to their clientele. For instance, they had socks with book patterns, quotes from famous books, and likenesses of authors.

After I'd met everyone, Mrs. Meacham handed me the keys to my shop and went upstairs. Although my shop wouldn't open until the first of September, she'd graciously given me this last week of August to get everything set up.

I unlocked my door and went inside. I was surprised to see Max standing by the window. I started to ask her how she'd got in, but then I saw that there was another door that led to the kitchen. I imagined my space had once been the family dining room. Anyway, it was apparent that the door between my space and the kitchen hallway had been left unlocked. I'd have to be careful to check that in the future.

But, for now, I didn't mind at all that Max was there. Or that it appeared she was wearing the same outfit she'd been wearing yesterday. Must have been some party!

"So, you leased the shop?" Max asked.

"I did!"

"Congratulations! I wish we could have champagne to celebrate."

I laughed. "Me too, but I'm driving."

Max joined in my laughter. "I'm so glad you're going to be here. I think we'll be great friends."

"I hope so." And I truly did. I immediately envisioned Max as my best friend—the two of us going to lunch together, talking about guys and clothes, shopping together. I reined myself in before I got too carried away.

I surveyed the room. The inside wall to my right had a fireplace. I recalled that all the rooms upstairs had them too. But this one had built-in floor-to-ceiling bookshelves on either side of the fireplace.

"Does this fireplace still work?" I asked Max.

"I imagine it would, but it isn't used anymore. The owners put central heat and air in eons ago."

"Just checking. I mean, I wasn't going to light fire to anything. I merely wanted to be sure it was safe to put flammables on these shelves." I could feel my face getting hot. "I'm sorry. That was a stupid thing to say. I'm just so excited—"

"And I'm excited for you. You have nothing to apologize for. How were you supposed to know whether or not the former tenant ever lit the fireplace?"

"You're really nice."

"And you're too hard on yourself. Must you be brilliant and well-spoken all the time?"

"Well...I'm certainly not, but I'd like to be."

"Tell me what you have in store for this place," she said.

I indicated the window. "I'd like to have a table flanked by chairs on either side here." I bit my lip. "Where's the best place around here to buy some reasonably priced furniture that would go with the overall atmosphere of the building?"

"I have no idea. You should ask Connie."

"Connie?" I was actually checking to make sure I'd heard Max correctly, but it so happened that I'd left the door open and Connie was walking by as I spoke.

"Yes?"

"Max was telling me that you might know of a good furniture place nearby," I said.

"Max?" Connie looked about the room. "Who's Max?"

I whirled around, thinking Max had somehow slipped out of the room. But, nope, there she stood...shaking her head...and putting a finger to her lips.

"Um...she was....she was just here. She was here yesterday too. I assumed she was a Shops on Main regular."

"I don't know her, but I'd love to meet her some-time. As for the furniture, I'd try the antique stores downtown for starters. You might fall in love with just the right piece or two there." She grinned. "I'd better get back to minding the store. Good luck with the furniture shopping!"

Connie pulled the door closed behind her as she left, and I was glad. I turned to Max.

"Gee, that was awkward," she said. "I was sure you knew."

"Knew?"

"That I'm a ghost."

Interested in reading more? Designs on Murder, Book One in the Ghostly Fashionista Mystery Series, at Grace Abraham Publishing (https://www.graceabrahampublishing.com) or wherever e-books, paperback books, or audiobooks are sold.